AMBER FIRE

AMINAT SANNI-KAMAL

First Published in Great Britain in 2023 by
LOVE AFRICA PRESS
103 Reaver House, 12 East Street, Epsom KT17 1HX
www.loveafricapress.com

Text copyright © Aminat Sanni-Kamal, 2023
All rights reserved.

No part of this publication may be reproduced, stored or transmitted in any form by any means, electronic, mechanical, photocopying or otherwise, without the prior permission of the publisher, except in the case of brief quotations embodied in reviews.

The right of Aminat Sanni-Kamal to be identified as author of this work has been asserted by them in accordance with the Copyright, Design and Patents Act, 1988

This is a work of fiction. Names, places, events and incidents are either the products of the author's imagination or used fictitiously. Any resemblance to actual persons, living or dead, is purely coincidental.

ISBN: 978-1-914226-40-3

Available in eBook and paperback

DEDICATION

To you who want to love and be loved —
"It is not time or opportunity that is to determine intimacy; - it is disposition alone. Seven years would be insufficient to make some people acquainted with each other, and seven days are more than enough for others."
—Jane Austen

ACKNOWLEDGMENTS

Writing a book is a journey that requires the support, encouragement, and contributions of many individuals. As I reflect on the completion of this project, I am filled with gratitude for the people who have helped me along the way.

First, I want to express my deepest appreciation to my family. Your unwavering belief in me and constant encouragement have been my pillars of strength throughout this endeavor. Thank you for understanding the long hours I spent hunched over my keyboard, lost in the world of words.

Tobechukwu, for all the times I sent you this story to review and all the times I came to you when I doubted myself, for your kind words, your acceptance, and your patience, thank you. A friend like you is rare. Your understanding, words of encouragement, and acts of service were invaluable in keeping me motivated and focused.

I am eternally grateful to Kiru Taye for creating the platform that brought this book to life and showing young Nigerian writers like me that beautiful and heartwarming stories can also come out of Africa. The day I searched for "Nigerian romance authors" on Google and your name came out at the top was when a considerable part of my life changed. Your guidance and insights have been instrumental in shaping the direction of this book and other stories I have previously written. Your expertise and willingness to share your knowledge have been a beacon of light on my writing journey.

I also extend my gratitude to the team at Love Africa Press, especially Zee Monodee, for your meticulous editing and valuable suggestions that have polished this book to its best version. Working with an editor like you who truly understands romance is invaluable. Your dedication to quality is evident in each word and on every page.

Writing this book would not have been possible without knowing that you, my readers, are there waiting to read it. Thank you for your curiosity and interest in this story.

Lastly and most importantly, no amount of gratitude is enough to Allah, I started writing this book when I was in a bad place with my faith, but when I finished, my faith in and relationship with Allah was stronger and better than ever. I am grateful for the lessons, the challenges, the growth, and the gift of writing beautiful stories.

To all those mentioned and those who remain unnamed but no less appreciated for their support, guidance, and inspiration, thank you from the bottom of my heart.

With heartfelt gratitude,
Aminat Sanni-Kamal

PROLOGUE

Ọya's Curse

Timi Ọlófà-iná

I curse you this day to spend the rest of your life filled with rage

For your betrayal, you will not know peace or happiness

You shall know only greed and hate

Your hate will consume you in this life and in every other life you live.

This curse can only be broken the day we meet again

And that day shall be the day you cease to exist in any of the realms.

CHAPTER ONE

Ìlú Òrìṣà
(City of the Gods)

The unthinkable had happened.

Ṣango, God of thunder and lightning, was still trying the wrap his head around it. One minute, he'd had his Oṣé in his hand, playing with it; the next, it was gone.

Had he dozed off for a second?

He shook his head. No, it wasn't possible. He didn't fall asleep except when he wanted to.

So, how had he dozed off? Most importantly, how had his Oṣé, his double-bladed axe that represented his authority and served as his battle weapon, disappeared from his hand? His Oṣé — created from the wood of a thousand-year-old Ìrókò tree, its blades forged by the Alágbẹ̀dẹ Òrìṣà, divine blacksmiths on the orders of Olódùmarè in the hottest part of the divine forge — proved small and light enough for him to carry about. Then once in battle, it extended, carrying the weight of the Ìrókò tree from which its handle was made and the heat of the forge from which its blade were crafted. It was a most formidable weapon only he could bear. But he hadn't had use for it in this form in a long time because there were no longer wars. So, he always conveniently had it on his person. Well, until now.

It couldn't have been stolen because nobody could touch it except him—anyone who dared would have their blood dry up instantly and die on the spot. As he paced about his outer Chambers, his forehead furrowed in worry, his robe making a swash sound as he absently dusted it.

The peacocks lazily strolling in his gardens caught his eye, and he paused to watch them over the terrace carved from warm-coloured marble. A soft, radiant luminescence emanated in the atmosphere as lush greenery cascaded down the edges of the terrace, flowing seamlessly to merge with the colourful green of his gardens. The sky was bright—it was always bright here, the blue of the skies sharper, the light from the sun more golden, and when night came, the silvery shine from the moon spread over the whole of Ìlú Òrìṣà like an enchantress.

Water gushed rhythmically from the mythical fountains in his gardens, adding to the allure of the perfumed flowers and infusing the air with magic. Wisdom, power, and magic were part of the atmospheric makeup of Ìlú Òrìṣà, and the scent of them hung thickly around the abodes of higher Òrìṣà.

Ṣango, regardless of his predicament, couldn't resist a smile as his peacocks with their iridescent feathers walked majestically to the rhythm of the fountains, the rhythm of magic. With each step, each dance, they echoed the heartbeat of life and creation. They reminded him of Ọṣun, goddess of love, beauty, and fertility, and also his ex-wife. He smiled at the fond memory of her turning into a peacock so she could fly to the highest point of the heavens to meet with Olódùmarè, the creator of All. He had thought her efforts pathetic at the time, but Olódùmarè had judged otherwise and rewarded her tenacity. Ọṣun was now the only deity who had direct access to Olódùmarè, the only messenger of the Supreme deity.

A scoff escaped him. How ironic that he couldn't love Ọṣun the way she wanted to be loved when she was the goddess of love. Ọya, the wife he did love, had betrayed him in ways he didn't want to think of for the rest of his eternal life. As deity, and formerly a human king, he was used to betrayal, but Ọya's had almost ruined him. Though he had healed from it — centuries of being alive ensured that — his heart still bore the scars. Some might say he deserved it; Ọṣun most definitely had. But a broken heart was still a broken heart.

He shook his head slightly as he resumed his pacing, then a sudden thought made him pause and look skyward.

Was this Olódùmarè's doing?

The Supreme usually left the deities to their caprices. They didn't like to get directly involved in the lives of the gods, much less those of humans, except when They believed Their authority as the Supreme was being threatened. Then under the guise of teaching humility, They would meddle with things.

It's what They had done so many years ago, back when deities— Òrìṣà —and humans had shared the same sky. Olódùmarè had caused a terrible drought to overcome the land. There had been nothing the deities could do about it. Frustrated their prayers were not being answered, stupid humans began to offer human sacrifices, a thing that hadn't been asked of them…and the beginning of a terrible depravity.

Ọṣun had taken it upon herself to speak directly to Olódùmarè at that point, to plead with Them to end the drought. It had been a perilous journey even for a goddess as powerful as Ọṣun, and she had almost dissolved, but it had been worth it at the end.

Ṣango blinked. Was this one of those periods where Olódùmarè felt threatened and wanted to reinforce Their authority as the Supreme?

"My Lord," a voice said.

Ṣango turned to see his trusted friend Gbonka standing behind him.

"Ah, Gbonka, you are here." He smiled and placed his hands on the general's broad shoulders.

"You sent for me." Gbonka lifted an eyebrow, no doubt surprised at his subtle tone and sudden show of affection.

"Yes. Yes, I did." Ṣango nodded then sighed. He opened his mouth to speak, though he didn't know how to say it.

"Is anything the matter, my Lord?"

"You are not here as my guard; you are here as my friend. You can drop the honorifics."

Upon those words, his oldest friend relaxed his shoulders and leaned casually against the bannisters.

"Fine, then, Ṣango. What is the matter? I was in the middle of training when your servant came to me, so this better be good."

"Something is wrong indeed," Ṣango admitted. "But it is not something I can say out here. The walls have ears and the wind carry whispers. I am not going to risk one of those wavering spirits listening in." He then stalked off into his inner Chambers.

His maidservants bowed as he walked past them. He ignored them in his usual fashion. When they attempted to follow him inside, he waved his hand in dismissal. He wanted to have a private conversation with Gbonka, who followed him begrudgingly into the room and shut the vast oak doors behind him.

"So—"

"My Ọṣẹ is missing," Ṣango blurted out, interrupting whatever Gbonka had been about to say and throwing away all the arrogant demeanour he always carried in the presence of others.

"What?!" Gbonka's eyes widened in a mix of astonishment and horror. "Ṣango, my Lord, this is not something to joke about."

"Does it look like I'm joking?" His expression must be a mirror of his friend's horror. He was infamous for his short temper, and Gbonka knew better than to aggravate him by assuming he could make a joke about something as serious as this.

His Ọṣẹ, though not connected to his powers as the god of thunder, lightning, and fire, was a gift from Olódùmarè and a part of him. Losing it would make him a laughing stock amongst deities, but it also had grave consequences because a gift from the Supreme deity was equivalent to a promise. An oath. Losing it was akin to breaking said oath, and in Ṣango's case, it meant he wasn't worthy of being a deity. The more thought of it made him feel pathetic. He hadn't felt this way since he was human, and the unused emotion felt like alien invention to his essence.

Gbonka sighed and took a seat at the small table opposite Ṣango's gigantic bed. The way he furrowed his brows, Ṣango couldn't tell whether he was being sceptical or tired, since he had been at the training grounds before he summoned him, or maybe both. Not that Ṣango could blame him if it were the former; even he found it difficult to believe that the symbol of his authority was gone.

Too restless to sit, he continued pacing the intricately designed hardwood, dark-toned floors of his inner chamber. The motifs carved into the planks were a detailed illustration of his symbols: Lightning and Fire.

"How did it happen?" Gbonka asked finally.

"I don't know," he replied honestly.

"You don't know." Gbonka shot to his feet, staring at him in disbelief. "You do know that Timi Ọlófà-iná could attack your palace at any moment. The news of the impending battle between you two is all Ìlú Òrìṣà is talking about. Do you know what would happen should the news of the disappearance of your Oṣé ever leave these four walls?"

"I would become an object of mockery. I know that." Ṣango felt a slight tingling sensation in his eyes as thunder rumbled outside. Anyone looking at him would see his eyes flash like he was about to set them on fire.

"Put a leash on your temper, Ṣango. Except if you want me here as your soldier and not your friend." Gbonka rolled his eyes. They had been friends for so long that Ṣango's mood swings and temper didn't faze him anymore.

Ṣango closed his eyes and took a deep breath to calm himself. Even he knew his temper was both a blessing and a curse, but he would never admit the latter to anyone else.

"Even without my Oṣé, Timi cannot take my place. He can only try," he said when he opened his eyes, dismissing Gbonka's fear.

"I don't think you should underestimate Timi. You may not have noticed since you keep winning the battle between you two all the time. But, with every battle he loses, he comes back stronger. He won't repeat the mistakes he made in the past, and he is very much determined to take your place. And by losing your Oṣé, you have no right to be here. He can use that against you."

"Oh, please, I am Ṣango. Nobody can take my place, especially not a simpering fool like Timi."

"At least, unlike you, he still has his weapon."

Ṣango sighed at Gbonka's retort. He was right—Timi still had his Ọfà-iná. What a disgraceful thing indeed. If news of his missing Oṣé ever got out, there wouldn't even be a battle: he would be a fallen god, and he couldn't let that happen.

He was the great and mighty god of thunder and fire—he would never let himself become a fallen god.

"Tell me everything from the beginning," Gbonka said as he sat back down. The crease on his forehead showed how distraught and concerned his oldest friend was for him.

Ṣango threw his hands up and shook his head. He didn't know where to begin.

"There isn't much to tell. I sat right where you were sitting, polishing my Oṣé, and I dozed off for what might have been a second, and the next thing I know, my weapon is gone. Whether it vanished into thin air or was snatched from my hands, I can't say."

Gbonka's turn to sigh, and he furrowed his brows even deeper and tilted his head slightly to the side as if a thought had occurred to him.

"Well, we can rule out the option of someone snatching it out of your hands. Everyone knows that's impossible, but it vanishing into thin air is even more unlikely unless...."

"Unless what?" Ṣango asked, his anxiety piqued by the look on his friend's face.

"My Lord, you said you dozed off," Gbonka said, getting to his feet, and Ṣango gave an impatient nod, eager to hear whatever theory Gbonka had come up with.

"You never doze off, you are never tired, you sleep only because you want to. It's usually a deliberate effort with you, and even when you do, you are still conscious of your surroundings."

"Skies, Gbonka, I know this about myself."

"It would mean there's a higher power at play here. Do you think maybe Olódùmarè had something to do with it?"

Ṣango rolled his eyes inward.

"I already considered that," he began, unable to hide the disappointment in his voice. "But it's most unlikely. Olódùmarè only interferes with our lives when They are bored or feel Their authority as the Supreme is being threatened. They have no reason to do that to me."

"They have every reason to do that with you," Gbonka countered.

"Why? I don't have any business with Them, neither do I wish to —"

"That's the first problem. You are apathetic, and you are not particularly subtle either. I mean, you walk around calling yourself mighty —"

"But I am mighty." Ṣango stared at his friend, incredulous.

"Nobody doubts that, Ṣango, but whenever They get like this, there is no reasoning with Them. But all of this is only an assumption that Olódùmarè is even involved with it all," Gbonka finished.

"So, how do we even know what is going on? I must find my Oṣé before word gets out it's gone. We can't keep on speculating. We need real answers."

"There is only one way to be sure if the Supreme is involved in this."

"Then tell me," Ṣango demanded.

Gbonka sighed and straightened, to look directly into Ṣango's eyes — one of the few people who could do that.

"I'll tell you, but you won't like it."

"Does it look like I'm in a position to be choosy?" Ṣango snapped.

"Fine, then, my Lord. The only way we can be sure of what's going on is to ask the one who has direct access to the Supreme."

Ṣango stared at his friend for a moment then burst out laughing, and in the same minute, all laughter cleared from his voice and face as he spoke.

"Tell me you are joking." The words came out laden with ice.

"I am not, my Lord."

"You do not possibly expect me to ask Ọṣun for help? It goes against my mightiness and—"

"I thought you said you were not in the position to be choosy." Gbonka stared at him stoically.

Ṣango hissed and sat down for the first time since they'd entered the inner Chambers.

"She hates me. You know that. If she comes to know of this, and if it turns out that the Supreme Deity is not involved, then it would have been better if I had stood on the highest mountain and announced my situation to the whole world myself."

"True," Gbonka agreed. "But you do not have any other choice."

"Fine," Ṣango agreed, resigned. "Do we know where she is at the moment?"

"No, but I can find out."

"I am sorry to have to ask you to do this, but you understand the severity of the situation."

"I understand, my Lord. It is always an honour to serve you." Gbonka gave a curt bow.

"Good, find her and bring her to me. Take my ẹdun àrá with you. It is the only way she would come with you."

Gbonka nodded and bowed again before leaving to do his bidding. Though Ṣango could tell by his rigidity that he wasn't too pleased to touch his thunder stone and even more displeased to find the goddess of love.

Ṣango was taking a big gamble by summoning Ọṣun, because whether or not Olódùmarè was involved, bringing Ọṣun into the matter didn't bode well for him.

CHAPTER TWO

Toyin sat at the table that had been reserved for this special occasion. She was sure it must be one. Tonight, Ṣẹyẹ was going to propose to her after seven years of dating. They had been together since her third year in university. A proposal was long overdue and merely a formality between them — they already knew they were getting married. They discussed it from time to time, talked about how many children they wanted to have — two boys and two girls.

They spoke about how the boys would look like their father, the girls like their mother, and where they would go for their honeymoon. Everything was set and perfect. They would have gotten married a few years ago, but Ṣẹyẹ had been unemployed for almost three years after graduating, and although her income as a scrub nurse was enough for them to get by, it wasn't enough to settle as a newlywed couple.

And now, things were different. Ṣẹyẹ was a manager in a bank and earned more than enough. The only issue they had? He wanted her to quit her job and become a full housewife when they got married, and she wasn't comfortable with it. On the contrary, she was thinking of going back to school to become a surgeon. She had nothing against full housewives — it just wasn't for her.

She didn't like how he suddenly wanted her to be dependent on him, knowing her life's story and how ambitious she was, but he loved her, and she loved him, and they would work it out. They'd had their issues over the years, and they had always sorted it out because they loved each other.

She looked up as someone walked into the restaurant and sighed in disappointment when it wasn't Ṣẹyẹ. She peeked at her phone; he was fifteen minutes late. The waiter had asked her twice now if she was ready to order.

She was already self-conscious as things stood. It felt like everyone in the restaurant was looking at her with pity — the gorgeously dressed woman being stood up.

Ṣẹyẹ wouldn't do this to her. He was the one who'd made the reservation. They hardly went to expensive places like this, so asking her on a date to such an exquisite restaurant could only mean he was ready to propose and wanted to make it memorable for her. Besides, she had seen the ring — he'd thought he'd hidden it well enough at the top of the wardrobe in his room, yet she had found it while searching for a document she thought she had left back at his place a couple of weeks ago.

Since then, she'd been riddled with anxiety, waiting for the day he would finally ask her. She'd tried calling him, but he wasn't picking up. She looked down at her phone again. Five more minutes, then she would leave.

And God help him if he didn't have a good explanation for standing her up like this.

Just as she made the decision, the door opened, and she glanced up expectantly. This time, there he was, looking handsome as ever, walking purposefully towards her.

"I'm so sorry, the meeting went on for longer than I expected and then I got caught up in Lagos traffic," he apologised.

Toyin wasn't having it.

"You could have at least picked up your phone when I called or sent me a text that you'd be late," she shot back at him as he took his seat.

"You've been calling…" he trailed as he brought his phone from the inner pocket of his suit jacket and checked it. "I can't believe this. I left it on DND since the meeting and completely forgot about it." He looked up at her. "You know I won't leave you here like this, my baby."

He then smiled at her and gently placed his hands over hers on the table.

That was all it took for her anger to dissolve. She could never win against his smile, and he knew it. Besides, how could she continue being angry when he had already apologised?

Seeing that her date had arrived, the waiter came again and this time took their order. He returned a few minutes later with their wine choice, filled their glasses, and then left to see to their dinner.

"You know today's supposed to be a special night for us. That's the only reason I'm letting you off the hook." Smiling back at him, she took a sip from her glass.

"Tonight's special?" Ṣẹyẹ asked, looking curious and a bit amused. "Do you have something planned for me after this?" he added with a mischievous glint in his eyes.

She laughed aloud and then quickly covered her mouth with her hands when she realised how loud she had sounded. A few heads turned to look at her, and she cleared her throat to hide her embarrassment. Ṣẹyẹ was pulling her leg. Obviously, he wouldn't tell her he was about to propose since it was meant to be a surprise.

"Fine, I'll pretend like I didn't know beforehand, so get on with it," she said, smiling as she dangled her left fingers in front of him.

"Get on with what?" he asked in genuine curiosity.

She understood he was trying to surprise her, but she had waited seven years for this moment, and she was too excited to get through the rest of the evening pretending she didn't know what he was about to do.

"Oh, come on, Ṣẹyẹ. I already saw the ring." She smiled broadly at him. "I didn't mean to snoop around your house, but I was looking for the—" She stopped talking when she saw the crestfallen look on his face. "Why do you look so sad? Is it because I ruined the surprise? We both know where this night is heading—we talked about it so many times, talked about getting married and having children and building a life together, and you asked me to meet you at this expensive restaurant which is so out of character for you. I bought this dress so I could look the part." She tugged at her burnt orange dress for emphasis. "I'm sorry I ruined it, but I am just too excited to wait."

She'd stumbled over her words and now wished so terribly she had kept quiet and let the evening flow on its own. Ṣẹyẹ liked to be in control, and she had most likely upset him by jumping the gun.

"Relax, Toyin," he said finally. "I returned the ring. I didn't know you had seen it."

She couldn't believe what she'd just heard. "You did what?"

"I thought you weren't ready. We argued about this a few weeks ago, and you said you weren't ready to quit your job. So, I thought you needed more time, and I returned the ring because we could use the money to do something else while we waited for you to make a decision."

Toyin's eyes widened in disbelief as she fixed her gaze on him. She most definitely wasn't hearing right. He had probably come to their date drunk. It was the only reason he could be saying such nonsense.

"So let me get this straight. Us getting married is dependent on whether or not I quit my job? Ṣẹyẹ, we have been together for seven years. You know my dreams, my ambitions. You, of all people, know why I had to settle for nursing when I really wanted neurosurgery. In all these years, you never mentioned that you wanted a wife who would be dependent on you. So, where's all these coming from?"

"I didn't have a job back then. Hell, I didn't even know what I wanted back then. Now, I have a job, and I want to work my way up to the highest level. I could even become CEO, but it would mean I have to work hard, and it would take a lot of my time. I can't have a wife who's equally as busy. You want to go back to school to study neurosurgery. That's going to take many years, and when you eventually start working, who am I going to come home to? Who's going to take care of the kids? Think about it, Toyin."

"You want me to give up my dreams so you can pursue yours? That's basically what you are telling me, Ṣẹyẹ."

It had to be a horrible nightmare, one she needed to wake up from immediately. Wanting her to quit her job was one thing, but for such a selfish reason was another.

"Not all of your dreams. It's been one of your biggest dreams to marry and have a big family, something you never had as a kid."

"Wow." She looked at him, and for the first time in seven years, she saw him for who he really was—a selfish, conceited bastard.

"Look, our dinner is here. Let's just have a pleasant evening like I intended," he said as the waiter brought their food while she stared at him dumbfounded and in a new light.

"When you think about it, you'll realise this is the best option for you. Going back to school is quite expensive, and I know you think you have saved enough to at least begin, but how do you intend to finish? You still have to support your mother. Why don't you let me do all the work, and you will get to live in luxury. Isn't that what this is all about, in the end? Wealth, recognition?"

"You know damn well this is more than that to me," she yelled at him. She no longer cared about how the other people in the restaurant saw her. She was a fool, a big one, and the whole world might as well know it.

"Toyin, why are you being like this?" he asked in a tone she used to think of as calm and soothing but now recognised as patronising. "You know how much I love you, and I know you love me just as much. I'm not asking for too much. I simply want a supportive wife, that's all."

"Hmm." She nodded sarcastically. "So when you finally make it and become this hotshot CEO, you'll be introduced as Mr CEO, but I won't even get the benefit of being a Dr (Mrs), even though I find that title quite ridiculous. You want to take everything from me, my last name, my ambitions, and even my unborn children in exchange for the benefit of being called your wife, abi?"

"Toyin, saying it like—" he began in his condescending tone.

"This Toyin, Toyin, you keep calling, do you even know my full name?" she asked him pointedly.

He scoffed. "What a ridiculous question, Oluwatoyin—"

"Wrong answer. Ṣangotoyin. That's my full name."

She got to her feet, considering for a second to empty the rest of her glass on his head but decided against it because he wasn't even worth it.

"If you have ever paid careful attention to the woman you want to be your wife, you would have known. My mother is from a family of Ṣango worshippers. My grandmother gave me this name, and although I have never really cared much for religion or deities, at this moment, right now, I wish Ṣango would strike you dead. You selfish bastard."

As soon as the words fell out of her mouth, lightning flashed across the night sky, followed by a loud rumbling of thunder and immediately a heavy downpour.

But Toyin was too angry to care. She stormed outside into the rain, leaving behind her dinner and a dumbfounded ex-boyfriend.

CHAPTER THREE

Ọṣun sauntered into Ṣango's inner chambers. No mistaking the smug look on her face, and she did little to hide the satisfaction that Ṣango finally needed her help.

Following closely on her heels was Gbonka, who shut the giant oak doors behind him and stood as far away as he could from the goddess. His rigid stance told how uncomfortable he was in her presence. She was the goddess of love, after all, and even gods weren't immune to her charms. One look was all it took for them to fall under her spell and devote their entire lives to her.

No one except Ṣango—ironic because he was the only one she had genuinely fallen in love with.

"My Lord." She gave a mock bow.

Ṣango resisted the urge to roll his eyes at her all so blatant mockery. She was still as beautiful as ever, in a sheer white dress, no doubt intending to distract him. The garment fell slightly off her shoulders and had slits so high, her inner thighs were exposed with every step she took. Back in the day, he would not have been able to resist her shimmering brown skin, which had led him to mistake the lust he'd felt for her body for love.

Love—such a ridiculous concept that shouldn't even exist. It gave men and gods alike the excuse to do stupid things.

"Let us cut the pretence and sarcasm. You are not that glad to see me," he said without getting up from his seat at his table. He gestured to her to sit with him. She smiled ever so sweetly at him as she took a seat.

Gone were the days when he could be taken in by her beautiful face and smile. He glanced at Gbonka, telling him with his gaze not to leave. He considered asking him to sit, but his friend would not sit beside the goddess even if his life depended on it.

"I would have offered you a drink, but I am sure you understand the severity of the situation does not leave room for pleasantries," he said to her.

"I do not know of any situation," Ọṣun replied. "Only that you sent your guard to me with your ẹdun àrá, making it impossible for me to refuse."

The glint in her eyes told him she knew exactly what the situation was, and she was enjoying every bit of his frustration.

"Surely, Gbonka must have explained it all to you." He humoured her.

"No, he did not," she replied, playing his game. "What is so urgent that you would send for a wife you rejected?"

"I did not reject you. You left of your own free will," Ṣango countered. He was taking her bait, and he didn't like it.

"Well, when you promise to love a woman and then proceed to love another instead, it is not only rejection but betrayal. And also, I was not going to wait around and let you turn me to ashes with your temper," she answered lazily, relaxing against the chair.

"I already apologised, for both incidents. What else do you desire of me?"

Ọṣun scoffed. "Your apology is as sincere as Eṣu promising to be straightforward."

This time, Ṣango did roll his eyes. As if the trickster god would ever play straight. He didn't have time to banter with Ọṣun. She was no longer angry or even hurt by what had happened thousands of years ago; she just wanted to rub it in that he needed her help after all these years.

"So, is the Supreme involved?" he asked impatiently, abruptly steering the topic to what was important to him.

"Involved in what?"

"In the disappearance of my Oṣé," he yelled out angrily.

Ọṣun gasped and covered her mouth in fake surprise.

"Your Oṣé disappeared? You, the mighty one, lost the symbol of your authority?"

"You cannot help yourself, can you?" Ṣango hissed. There was no need to get angry at her. After he had burned down his palace all those years ago out of anger, all three of his ex-wives had become immune to his fluctuating temper.

"But it is funny, do you not think so, too?" she asked, turning to Gbonka, though his friend gave no response—his face remained stoic, and he looked almost as if he were holding his breath; Ṣango couldn't be sure.

"Ọṣun, this is not the time to joke. Tell me if you know anything at all," he pleaded.

The goddess sighed, and for the first time all evening, her face took on a severe expression. She tapped her fingers lightly on the polished mahogany round table as she seemed to study Ṣango's face before she spoke.

"Well?" Ṣango couldn't stand the suspense.

"What came for you is coming for all of us," she said finally, her voice a bit sad.

"What does that mean? I do not have time for riddles."

"You better be patient and listen carefully to what I have to say. This is something only the Supreme and I know of, and now, you, too, will know about it. I allow Gbonka to be here because I know he would rather die than betray you."

"Well, he did die than betray me," he corrected her.

"The world of the deities is ending," Ọṣun said, ignoring his correction.

"What?" Ṣango raised an eyebrow slightly, showing his disbelief. "That is only possible when humans forget completely about us. Do you know how many humans roam the earth? Every single human cannot forget about the existence of the deities."

"True," Ọṣun agreed and then stared directly into his eyes. "It is impossible, except there is some sort of divine catalyst."

Ṣango nodded, slowly absorbing the information Ọṣun was giving him.

"You are the catalyst," she said pointedly.

Those words shocked him, and he was hardly ever surprised by anything.

"Me? Do not joke with me. I have not involved myself in the lives of humans for centuries. I have been here in my palace in the comfort of my servants and loyalists. The only conflict I have had in centuries is with Timi—"

"The genesis of your conflict with Timi is the problem," Ọṣun stated, interrupting him.

"What do you mean?"

"Gbonka is a demi-god because he died for you when we still lived under the same sky as humans, right?"

Ṣango nodded and gestured for her to go on.

"Well, Timi also became a demi-god because you murdered him with hatred in your heart for him, and he died with hate in his heart for you.

His goal when he was human was to take your place as king of the human world, but he died because he was a mere human going against a god. Now that he is a demi-god, his goal is to become a god, specifically the god of thunder and fire, and that is only possible if he kills you."

She still wasn't making much sense to him.

"Two humans became demi-gods on your account," Ọṣun continued. "One was because of his love for you, and the other was born out of his hatred for you. All Timi's effort over the years to usurp you has proven futile, and the only way he could think of to get rid of you is to make humans forget you."

She paused here. Ọṣun didn't like to talk a lot; she passed her message in single sentences or phrases. It was also one of the things that had attracted him to her — she listened more than she spoke, but this situation was different. A dire situation that affected her life as a deity, too.

"But that is impossible. I have worshippers all over the world, and Timi is merely a demi-god whose existence hangs on the hatred he has for me. He cannot pull off such a feat."

"Of course he cannot. That is why he sought help from Eṣu."

"Why in the name of the skies would anyone want to have dealings with Eṣu òdàrà? Even his human worshippers are careful in their dealings with him."

"Only a desperate person would go to such lengths."

"What did he promise Eṣu in return for this stupid thing?" Ṣango asked, curious to know what his life was worth.

"That is the funny part of this whole thing. Your battle with Timi always ends with you winning. It is the biggest source of entertainment in the world of deities. Eṣu got bored with you always winning. He wanted something different and more exciting, so he agreed to tip the odds. He is one of the few gods powerful enough to cast a glamour over the minds of humans, and with how fickle the minds of humans are of late, it worked perfectly. The problem is that it worked too perfectly. It was supposed to be a temporary glamour, but it became a permanent one that is slowly wiping away not just you out of the memory of humans but all other deities."

Ṣango strained so hard to restrain his anger because one of the things he had learned, living for as long as he had, was that anger hardly ever resolved things, and in this case, it certainly wouldn't make humans remember him.

"I cannot believe Eṣu did all this nonsense for entertainment. He sometimes forgets the extent of his powers and does things on a whim. If there is anyone I should be angry with, it is Orí. I am sure he must have seen all this before it happened," Ṣango spat.

"You cannot blame Orí either. Even the god of destiny cannot interfere with destiny; he can only see it. He cannot and must not change it," Ọ̀ṣun replied and narrowed her eyes at him in a warning.

If he were blaming Orí, he would blame Olódùmarè next for overlooking things; all deities got their nonchalance from Them.

"What is the solution? What do we have to do to change this?" he asked.

"The only solution to this is for you to find the one human who still believes in you, the human who would love you as much as Gbonka did. A human who can die for you," Ọ̀ṣun answered grimly.

Even she knew how difficult the task was. Humans like Gbonka were rare. They believed it was a deity's duty to die for them and not the other way round. Their selfish nature made it hard for them to love so deeply. It would be even more difficult now that their belief in gods was seeping away.

"Timi and Èṣù created this mess. I do not know why I am the one who has to clean it up," Ṣàngó muttered.

"You have thirty days, going by the time of humans," Ọ̀ṣun stated.

He threw his hands up.

Trust the Supreme to include an impossible time frame into the whole drama. After all, if humans forgot about the deities, it was only a matter of time before they forgot about Them, too. But, They could also easily find his Oṣé and return it to him, but They would instead make a statement about his worthiness: he was the one who had lost it, so he must be the one to get it back.

"While you are in the world of the humans, Olódùmarè will make it seem as if you have never left. No one will think to look for you or your trusted one. I am assuming you will be going with him?"

"Whether or not I go with Gbonka is not the problem. The problem is, how am I supposed to find a human who still believes in me among a sea of humans with a divine-induced memory loss?" Ṣango asked in a frustrated tone.

It so happened that the moment those words left his mouth coincided with the exact moment Toyin angrily and unintentionally invoked his wrath upon the man who had betrayed her.

Both Ṣango and Ọṣun grinned broadly, and even Gbonka managed a stiff smile at the perfect coincidence.

"This is Orí's doing. He is tweaking destiny slightly because this affects him just as it affects you. It affects all of us. The fate of Ìlú Òrìṣà now hangs on your shoulders," Ọṣun said.

For the first time since the disappearance of his Oṣé, his task had become a whole lot easier. All he had to do was follow the scent of the

human's aura and make her love him enough to
die for him.

CHAPTER FOUR

'Unbreak my Heart' by Toni Braxton had been on repeat on the highest volume for the last three days in Toyin's apartment. She was most likely being a nuisance and disturbing her entire neighbourhood, but not like they could report her to the police. This was Lagos, not the United States; everyone was a nuisance to each other in this city. Besides, none of them were in her shoes, so they didn't know where it hurt.

She had taken a leave of absence for the first time in all the years she worked at the hospital. She was so dedicated to her work that she hardly ever took a break, even on holidays. This time, she'd had no choice. She couldn't assist in any surgeries—even if she did try, the operating surgeon would kick her out of the operating room. If that happened, she would either lose her job or be sent to jail. Either way, it would affect her plans to further her studies.

So, better she stayed at home and nursed her injured emotions before going back to work.

However, she didn't think she would ever be able to recover from this.

She'd finally come to her senses after about an hour of walking without a particular destination in mind that night and had taken a cab the rest of the journey back to her apartment. Not for the first time, she was happy to have moved out of her mother's home and into her own tiny flat. It was a rented space, but it was hers. She didn't have to deal with anyone poking their nose into her business. She loved her mother, but she couldn't deal with her infamous African mother policing, hence why she had gathered up the money to get her own place.

She laughed as she thought about how cliché she was when the song started playing all over again. Deciding to be as cliché as she could be, she turned off the music to binge-watch one of her favourite shows on Netflix instead.

Turning on her laptop, she was surprised to see it was quarter past seven in the evening. She was in the same spot on the floor in her tiny living room since she'd returned from the restaurant. She had only managed to peel the wet clothes off her skin and drop them somewhere in her house, put on her pyjamas, and press play on her heartbreak song. She only got up when she needed to pee, drink water, and then once to get her laptop from her bedroom. Even the approval of her four-week leave of absence had been done over the phone. Whenever she was feeling better, she would go to the hospital to have the necessary documents signed.

Maybe by then, she would have enough strength to deal with Nkem and Lola — her colleagues had been trying desperately to form a friendship with her. They weren't bad people, but she didn't have the energy for their type of friendship. They were extroverts who were always at one party or the other, and they knew almost everybody in the medical industry — how they had the time to do all that going out, mixing, and mingling with all their duties proved a mystery she would never be able to solve. They probably thought she was a snob, but she was just too introverted and self-conscious to be their friend. She loved her safe spaces. She'd thought she'd found one in Ṣẹyẹ. Just how well had that turned out.

Browsing through shows on Netflix, she heard the rumbling thunder.

What was with the weather in the middle of December when everyone was looking forward to that Christmas feeling? The decline in the environment had messed up the climate.

She shook her head slightly as she looked towards the pile of empty plastic bottles in the corner of the living room and that she knew she wasn't going to recycle. She would throw them in the trash can outside her apartment building; they would most likely end up in an open-air incinerator like the one at Ojota.

The sight brought to mind how she needed to clean her apartment. Even the wet clothes she had dropped off somewhere were beginning to give off a terrible odour. Thinking of wet clothes reminded her of the ones she had washed and spread out three days ago before her date, still outside on the line.

She had half a mind to leave them there. After all, they had gotten drenched in the rain once, but she wasn't so rich that she would let her clothes get soaked in the rain a second time.

With a resigned sigh, she pulled herself to her feet sluggishly, cursing the fickle weather. She went outside to take her clothes from the spread wire and cursed again as she descended the stairs.

"Why couldn't I have gotten the apartment on the ground floor?" she muttered to herself.

"Because nobody really wants the ground floor, especially in an old building like this one?" an unmistakably masculine voice said behind her.

The voice surprised her so much, she turned sharply, missed a footing on the stairs, and went flying down.

This was it — this was how she was going to die. Her tombstone would read:

"Here lies a miserable young woman who died without getting her boyfriend to marry her. Immediately before that, it would have said; *she failed to keep the promise she had made to her father on his deathbed. What a sad, terrible life she lived."*

"No, it will not say that because you will not be dying today."

Toyin opened her eyes to the realisation that she had been caught by the man who had startled her in the first place. She found herself staring into a pair of amber eyes. Suddenly breathless, she got lost in the beauty of his eyes for more than a moment, so much so, she didn't dwell too much on how the man had replied to her thoughts.

"I think you should let go of my shirt now. It is one of a kind," he said with an amused grin.

For a second, Toyin thought his unusual eyes flashed, but she had to be mistaken. Anyway, his words brought her back to her senses, and she instantly became self-aware.

She had always thought of the stairway as tiny, yet now, it felt extra cramped up with the imposing presence of this stranger with the bronze skin and cornrows. She gave him a once over from head to toe. He looked and smelled like money, and he didn't have the look of a man who lived in Nigeria. He was probably an IJGB home for the holidays.

The only bulb lighting up the stairway flickered, reminding her she was standing alone with a stranger.

"Wh... who are you?" she stuttered and backed up the stairs a little, although she would have to admit it was a bit too late for that. He would have harmed her already if that were his intention. Besides, he had stopped her fall.

How had he done it? She was pretty sure he'd been standing behind her. She didn't have time to ponder too long because he noticed her pathetic attempt at retreating and laughed.

Toyin didn't think she had ever heard laughter that sounded this beautiful before. She shook her head. What was wrong with her? It had to be the break up messing with her common sense. She should be in the safety of her apartment behind bolted doors because, for all she knew, he could be a predator assessing his prey.

He laughed again as if reading her thoughts, but this time, before she had the opportunity to make another comment, he answered the question she'd asked him earlier.

"I am your new neighbour. I just moved into the apartment opposite yours," he answered.

He had to be joking. That apartment had been empty in the four years she'd been living in the building. Nobody, whoever saw the apartment, wanted it. She had always thought it weird how no one wanted it when it was in perfectly good shape and cheap. Yet now, a weird guy was claiming he'd moved into it.

"The apartment being empty is Orí's doing. I am destined to live in that apartment for a short while and—"

"Wait a minute, I definitely did not say that out loud. Are you reading my thoughts?" she asked, her eyes widening in horror. She was sure she hadn't said those words out loud.

She backed up the stairs. Beautiful or not, she shouldn't be anywhere near this stranger.

"You need to stop trying to run away from me. I do not mean you any harm," he said, sounding amused, like he was watching a comedy show. "And," he said, taking a step towards her while she automatically backed up. "We need to address this whole being weird thing."

He had most definitely read her mind because she wasn't one to call people weird to their faces, no matter how they looked or acted. She didn't like to hurt people's feelings.

"Who are you?" she asked again. She hated how weak her voice sounded. She'd read somewhere that you should never show fear, no matter how afraid you were, or something like that.

"Fine. This is getting boring, anyway," he said with the air of a man who wasn't used to being asked who he was, and Toyin had asked that question several times in the past few minutes. "I am Ṣango, and I am here because you summoned me."

There — that quick flash of fire in his eyes.

Staring at him for a few seconds and seeing how the seriousness never left his face after such a ridiculous declaration, Toyin was now fully convinced a crazy guy had broken into her apartment building. Judging by how fast he had caught her when she was falling, she knew she could not outrun him.

So, she did the only thing she could think of at the moment.

She screamed.

CHAPTER FIVE

What in the name of the skies was wrong with her?

Even the peacocks in his gardens weren't as loud as this. If he hadn't heard Toyin invoke his wrath himself, he would have believed Ọṣun had intentionally sent him onto the path of a disturbed woman.

Ṣango stood still and watched while she screamed out her lungs, calling for help. Moving towards her would only aggravate her further.

Neighbours who heard her scream came out of their apartments, and the tiny stairway grew crowded in no time.

"Mr Ṣango," the stout, middle-aged, and balding agent who had rented out the apartment to him and who also thankfully lived in one of the units on the ground floor called him. "What is going on here?"

Ṣango cast him a side-eye but otherwise remained quiet. He wasn't the one causing the nuisance. Why should he be the one to answer the question?

Seeing the look on his face, the man turned away quickly. The agent was afraid of him. He had been since the first day they met, which meant his common sense was still working.

Ṣango leaned against the wall, casting a nonchalant gaze on the people in the crowd. The women, both young and old, eyed him lustfully while the men tried not to meet his gaze, obviously intimidated by his presence.

"Toyin, why, just why, are you screaming? Do you want the building to collapse?" the agent who had squeezed his way up to where Toyin had been screaming asked in an annoyed tone.

Toyin was saying something to the agent, but he couldn't hear them, the crowd's thoughts on the stairway interfering. They needed to go. Not as if they were here because they were concerned about her anyway. They were here so they could talk about the single woman who lived upstairs alone.

Why that was a reason to dislike someone was beyond him, but if being a god had taught him anything, it was that the ways of humans and their logic would forever be a mystery to him.

Their reasoning defied both logic and common sense. Like the issue of human sacrifice. Nobody in the realm of the deities could fathom how humans ever came up with the idea. A committee had been set up to devise a reason for such nonsense and concluded that humans loved bloodshed more than they cared to admit.

Tired of listening to their obscene thoughts, he straightened up and gave a single command. "Leave now, all of you."

And as if hypnotised, they all went back into their respective apartments without question.

They may be losing their belief in the existence of deities, but they dared not go against a god's word, especially one as mighty as Ṣango.

The stairway had quieted again, with only Toyin as the agent retreated. He hadn't willed the man to leave; his presence proved crucial for Toyin to believe he wasn't a psychopath. He'd learned the word from her thoughts.

"I'm sorry for the misunderstanding, Mr Ṣango," the house agent apologised.

Ṣango ignored him, and he didn't need to be told she felt sorry towards him. He could hear it in her thoughts and see it in the way she avoided looking at him.

Feeling the need to fill up the silence, the agent continued talking. "I have explained to her that you are her new neighbour and..."

Ṣango muted the man and continued to stare at Toyin.

She didn't need to feel sorry towards him. The world of humans was already so cruel to women, her reaction only to be expected. He would forgive her this time.

"That is fine, you may leave now," he said in a dismissive tone, and the man stopped talking, bowed, and left.

Even the agent couldn't tell why he had felt the need to bow to his new tenant, but Ṣango's presence and aura were so dominating, humans couldn't help but pay obeisance to him.

"I... I—" Toyin began her apology, but he interrupted her.

"You do not need to apologise." He then stalked off, leaving her tongue-tied, and just before he entered his apartment, he paused. "Do not forget your clothes. It really might rain, and I have done my best holding it back for you."

He said this without turning to look at her and then opened the door to his apartment, feeling her bewilderment burn into his back.

He smirked; he just couldn't help himself.

Inside, his apartment was a far cry from what the building looked like on the outside. He had been appalled when he and Gbonka had followed the thread Ọṣun had used to tether him to Toyin three days ago to this dilapidated sorry excuse of a building. He had been even more pissed when he'd been shown what was supposed to be the largest apartment inside it.

The place had been in a horrible state. A human shouldn't have to live there. Talk more of a god. There had been rats crawling all over the filthy space. When Orí had said he'd prepared a place for him because he knew this day was coming, and he'd made sure no human had stained it in five human years, he'd said it as if he had been doing him a favour.

If Ṣango dwelled on it too much, he would bring his wrath down on Orí, the mischievous little chit. But doing that was the same as bringing his anger on the whole world because if the god of destiny ceased to exist, the world would cease to exist. The bastard walked around doing whatever he liked because he knew no one could touch him, not even Ṣango, one of the most powerful deities.

The good thing about being a god? All he had to do was think, and everything he wanted would manifest in front of him. Just like that, he had turned this dump into a fancy apartment equipped with state-of-the-art facilities of the human world.

Lounging on the plush couch, he marvelled at the television like it was an alien artifact—funny he thought about this word, considering what he was in this world—or perhaps a mystical portal to another dimension. He had actually believed he could be transported back to his home if he touched or maybe broke it. Gbonka, who had been watching him quizzically as he tried to figure out the box, had stopped him from breaking it.

Now, he watched the sleek, flat-screened box that dominated the room exuding technological—another new word he'd learned—aura. Though the movements and colours on the screen proved enthralling and entertaining if he was being honest, he didn't think he could get used to watching humans speak, dance, or do whatever they do without being able to touch them or even speak to them.

But the television wasn't all that marvelled him in this new human world. There, sitting on the coffee table, was what Gbonka had called a smartphone. He found this even more fascinating than the television. He refused to acknowledge that he had flung the first one Gbonka had gotten him against the wall and smashed it when it first vibrated in his hands. In his defence, he'd thought the thing possessed, and who dared possess him? Its sleek design and touch-sensitive surface baffled him, and the idea that this tiny device held the knowledge of the entire human race was utterly mind-boggling. He shouldn't be too surprised, though, because if there's one gift Olódùmarè blessed humans with, it was the magic of innovation.

A whole lot had changed since he had last walked the Earth, and he and Gbonka had spent the first two days learning the ways of the new world. Thankfully, he was a fast learner, and he'd extended such grace to Gbonka, as well.

Speaking of whom, where in the skies had Gbonka disappeared to? He hadn't seen him all morning. He sighed and closed his eyes.

Gbonka!

By the time he opened his eyes, Gbonka was standing in front of him, a half-eaten fried chicken wing in his hand.

"My Lord," he protested. "We agreed you cannot do this here."

Ṣango wasn't smiling. "I was almost mobbed on that useless staircase, but my bodyguard was nowhere to be found."

"I highly doubt the possibility of that happening," Gbonka said as he snapped the chicken into two.

Ṣango turned his mouth down at him in disgust.

"Besides," Gbonka continued, taking a seat. "That is why we got cell phones. You cannot just summon me in this world because I cannot be disappearing in front of humans. Also, when you summoned me, I was in the middle of —"

"I met our human friend today," Ṣango interrupted him.

"Oh, she finally came out of her apartment," Gbonka replied and then paused as if observing something. "She has also stopped playing that infernal song. I thought it would never end."

Ṣango scoffed. That song had been the bane of both their existence since they had moved in. He wondered why she would listen to a tune over and over again.

No matter how much he loved the sound of the bata drum, he couldn't stand it if it played ceaselessly for days. But after meeting her today, he had finally found out why, yet he wasn't particularly sure he understood the meaning.

"What is a breakup?" he asked Gbonka.

"Obviously, when something breaks apart." Gbonka eyed him.

"My human subject is going through a breakup. It is why she is so sad. She seems completely whole to me. Needs to work on her personal hygiene, though. Does not look like she has had a bath in days. Other than that, she seemed fine to me. I do not see any broken parts in her," he said, and Gbonka rolled his eyes.

"My Lord, you are supposed to be a fast learner," he said and sucked loudly on the chicken bone.

Ṣango wanted to smack him across his head. He wasn't sure if the human world affected his manners or if his friend had always been this uncultured.

"I did not bring you here to be mocked," he warned, deciding to ignore the irritating way his friend was smacking his lips.

"You know how you split with all three of your wives. That is what a breakup is," Gbonka explained.

Ṣango nodded slowly as understanding dawned on him. "But I still do not get one thing. I was not as sad as my human subject when I split with my wives."

"You remember how you felt and how your fire died when Ọya did what she did?" Gbonka said, and Ṣango flinched. "Forgive me, my Lord. That was thoughtless of me." Gbonka bowed, realising he had made a colossal blunder.

It had indeed been thoughtless of him. No matter how long it had been, Ọya's betrayal was still an open wound.

Gbonka was his oldest friend and servant. A slip of the tongue was bound to happen one of these days. And it had made him understand what his human subject was going through.

"Gbonka." His voice came out low and dangerous.

"My Lord," Gbonka replied without daring to look up at him.

"You are too handsome to have such terrible eating manners."

Gbonka looked up at him, surprised he had chosen to ignore the mistake.

He gave half a smile. He wasn't going to punish his most trusted ally over something that had happened a long time ago, no matter how hurt he still was by it.

Besides, he was more interested in his human subject now he understood what she was feeling.

CHAPTER SIX

Toyin paced about her living room, too restless to sit down. It had to be a dream. It had all the elements of a dream.

First, no way in the world could a man be that handsome. It should be a sin for a man to look so gorgeous.

She'd never liked arrogant or cocky men. She'd never found it attractive, and this man wore those traits like a second skin. He had the air of a man who breezed through life because everything and everyone fell at his feet.

She wanted to fall at his feet.

Then, his eyes — those amber eyes that glowed whenever his emotions shifted in the slightest, it seemed.

And his name: Ṣango. What kind of parents named their child Ṣango? He didn't seem to have a prefix or a suffix attached to his name like hers. His parents must be so devout to the god of thunder and fire to name their child after him and have him believe he was a deity.

But that didn't explain how he read her mind and replied to her thoughts, or had she voiced them out without knowing?

Still, it didn't make sense. He'd dismissed all the neighbours with one sentence, and the house agent who walked about like he owned the world seemed afraid of him and had actually bowed to him.

Toyin turned her head slightly. She couldn't wrap her mind around it, and as if all these weren't bad enough, she'd met such a man when at her worst. She hadn't brushed her teeth or had a bath in the past three days, and she had a ketchup stain on her pyjamas.

Arhhhhh! Better if the ground opened and swallowed her. When Skibii had said "never to be caught unfresh," this was what he meant.

This man named Ṣango had most definitely caught her "unfresh." She had to rectify that. Why, though? What did she want from this strange man who walked around like he owned the earth? Was it his eyes? She would be lying if she said his amber eyes weren't mesmerising. Well, she could put that down to the fact not many people had his kind of eyes. Actually, she hadn't met anyone with his kind of eyes. Okay, but how would she explain the urge she had to touch, no, feel his butter-smooth skin? Or the crazy way her heart seemed to beat faster around him.

Nope. No. Nope. She shook her head as she paced. That was stupid. The heart palpitations were probably an effect of her broken heart. The *shege* and *wahala* Ṣẹyẹ had put her through were definitely enough to cause heart problems. He was her new neighbour, and neighbours should at least be cordial. So, it wouldn't do for him to think she was a crazy, dirty person.

She stopped pacing, now that she had a logical reason, and smiled to herself as a plan formed in her head. Her drama with her ex-boyfriend was forgotten momentarily as she dashed into her bathroom to begin the process of righting her wrongs.

***

Standing in front of his door with a bowl of spicy jollof rice and roast chicken, she reconsidered if this was a good idea, after all.

What if he didn't like jollof rice? That would be a shame because she had spent many hours in the kitchen preparing the food. It didn't sound proper to apologise to him empty-handed, and since she wasn't sure what one gave a new neighbour, she'd made her favourite dish as a peace offering instead.

She had already reached his door. She'd come this far. It would be pointless for her to turn back now. Besides, she was never really one to turn back from a fight. Taking in a deep breath, she pressed the doorbell.

Another man opened the door. She gave him a once over: a handsome one, tall, dark-skinned, with well-formed muscles. He was bare-chested, dressed only in slacks, and so she had the good fortune to ogle.

The man cleared his throat, obviously embarrassed by the way she was looking at him.

"Oh, I'm sorry. I think I'm at the wrong apartment," she apologised. She should leave, but the sight in front of her made her hesitate.

"No, you are not," the man answered. "I take it you are looking for Ṣango. Please come in," he added with a smile that deepened the dimples on his cheeks.

He was more cute than handsome, and she resisted the urge to press her finger against his dimples just to see how deep they went — she had to do something about her intrusive thoughts.

"Oh, oh, thank you," she said and stepped inside the apartment, immediately captivated by its pristine state.

Was this place in the same building she lived in? The black and white interior décor was out of this world. She might as well be in Heaven. She had only dreamed of ever entering a space like this. It was indeed the biggest apartment in the building, but how could it be the cheapest when it looked like a presidential suite? Something didn't add up.

"He is in the bathroom. He should be out shortly. Please make yourself comfortable."

The man's pleasant voice brought her out of her reverie.

"Thank you. I'm Toyin," she introduced herself, still holding the casserole in her hand.

"I am Gbonka, Ṣango's friend and bodyguard, and he has told me about you." He beamed at her.

Her cheeks flushed in embarrassment. Of course, he had told him about her and the drama she had caused the previous day.

"Nah, do not worry about it. Ṣango can be a bit overbearing," he assured her and winked, and she smiled.

"So, this is how you talk about your lord in his absence."

Ṣango's voice interrupted them, and Toyin turned to behold a breathtakingly gorgeous man. Gbonka paled in comparison to him.

She immediately felt hot, which was absurd because the room was fully air-conditioned. He looked fresh out of the shower. The tips of his cornrows were wet and dripped water down his neckline to his bare chest. He only had a white towel tied around his hips. Her lips and throat suddenly went dry.

How could a man look this delicious? She had only been attracted to one man in her entire life, but it didn't feel the same. What an abomination for it to feel the same.

Ṣango gave her a wicked grin. Was he reading her thoughts again?

"I... I wanted to apologise for how I behaved yesterday," she began as Ṣango studied her with an amused glint in his amber eyes. "I hope you like jollof rice and chicken. I didn't want to come empty-handed."

"Chicken?"

Gbonka's voice peaked up with excitement, and Ṣango rolled his eyes. Toyin smiled at Gbonka, who took the casserole from her hands.

"We will surely enjoy this, Toyin, I can assure you—"

"No, you cannot assure her of anything because you are leaving," Ṣango said in a matter-of-fact tone.

"No, I am not," Gbonka protested.

"Yes, you are. You are going to put that in the kitchen and then leave," Ṣango insisted in his calm tone, but the glare in his eyes seemed utterly dangerous.

Gbonka glared back at him for a second, and then with a resigned sigh, he headed to the kitchen with the casserole in his hand.

Toyin laughed, and Ṣango turned his piercing gaze back to her.

"I do not understand why you laugh," he said.

"You two are so cute," Toyin replied.

Ṣango looked affronted. "I have been called many things, but I have never been called cute."

She could only smile. This man was weird in every sense of the word—the way he spoke, how regal he looked, and he was obviously wealthy. So why did he choose to live in such a place when he could afford a better one?

Gbonka came back out, wearing a shirt this time and grumbling as he made his way out of the apartment. He looked every bit like a fussy child.

"I bid you a very good evening, Toyin," he said to her with a genuine smile on his face and then glared at Ṣango. "My Lord, please use the phone this time," he said to him and then stalked out.

Toyin wondered what that meant.

"Everyone seems to do your bidding all the time," she said to Ṣango as soon as Gbonka shut the door behind him.

"Are you going to stand like that all evening?" Ṣango asked her instead of answering her question.

"Are you going to stay shirtless like that all evening?" she shot back.

He proved distracting, to say the very least. Seeing him standing there, half-naked, a rush of electrifying sensations surged through her. The play of his chiselled muscles and the way the soft glow of the room accentuated his features sent her heart into a frenzied dance. At that moment, she mused again on what it would feel like to run her hands down those muscles, the thought alone increasing the jolts of electricity going through her body.

Forcing her eyes off his chest, to look at his face, the first thing that caught her gaze were his full lips curled in a sensual smile that made her wonder what he could do with his beautiful mouth.

What the hell was she thinking? This wasn't only wild; it was unfamiliar territory.

"I can make those fantasies of yours come true," he said and dragged her closer to him, knocking what was left of her breath out of her.

If looking at his bare chest had sent jolts of electricity through her, this felt like being strapped to an electric chair with her executioner having turned the voltage up to the highest level. Because she couldn't remember to breathe—was breathing even necessary?

Wrapping his arms around her waist, he pressed her body against him. She could feel his warm breath against her skin.

"You are so lovely," he whispered and planted a kiss on her cheek.

Toyin closed her eyes, enjoying the feel of his body pressed against hers. It was like snuggling under a warm blanket on a cold harmattan morning. His warmth sent a tingling sensation down her spine as he planted kisses on random parts of her body. The feel of his lips against her skin ignited a fire within her. She moaned with pleasure.

Her eyes flew open, the sound of her moaning bringing her back to her senses.

"We should stop," she said.

Ṣango immediately let go of her, although she could see the fire of the lust he felt for her still burning brightly in his amber eyes.

"Did I misread your thoughts?" he asked, backing away from her.

"No, no, you didn't," she said truthfully, but that was the problem. The fact that she'd only just met this man yesterday and had moved from being creeped out by him to being overwhelmingly overcome with lust for him proved questionable.

She had only been with one man all her life, and even then, it had taken two years of dating before she finally had sex with him. She wasn't a prude or anything like that, but she was the type of woman who liked to be sure before she went all the way.

And there was the issue of this man believing he was a god and how quickly she was accepting his ability to read her thoughts as normal…when it was anything but. Things were moving way too fast. Her curiosity had brought her here, and now…

"I'll answer all your questions. All you need to do is ask," Ṣango said to her.

He had that look in his eyes, like he were studying her, like a predator weighing out his prey, and somehow, she was turned on by it. It lit little fires all over her that she surprisingly didn't hate. She welcomed the feeling and wanted to explore it. But she didn't know this man, and nothing about the entire situation felt normal. She had to focus.

"First, you need to put on some clothes," she said and then moved to the couch, determined to put as much space as she could between the two of them. "I'll sit right here and wait for you because I have so many questions."

He grinned at her. "Fine, make yourself comfortable. I'll be right back."

He turned and went to his bedroom.

Toyin heaved a sigh of relief when he left and sank into the couch. Goodness, it was so comfortable, she couldn't remember if she had ever sat on something so luxurious and expensive in her whole life.

She spent hours on her feet in the hospital and returned to a tiny and cramped apartment. Even her boyfriend's—ex-boyfriend's—entire home couldn't compare to this single couch she sat on. She was sure this piece of furniture cost more than Ṣẹyẹ's total salary in one year.

Closing her eyes, she sank deeper into the cushions. The thoughts running through her mind just before she fell asleep stated she needed to know everything about the man who would put such an expensive couch in one of the cheapest buildings in Lagos.

The next time Toyin opened her eyes, she found herself tucked in under the cosiest covers in the most enormous bed she'd ever slept in. She burrowed deeper under the quilts, enjoying the feel, and would have fallen back asleep had she not heard someone chuckle.

A man was in her bedroom. Then it hit her: she wasn't in her bedroom, and her bed wasn't this big and definitely not this cosy. Her eyes flew wide open, and she sat up so fast, she grew light-headed.

"Relax, or you shall give yourself a headache."

She recognised the voice and the person it belonged to.

She was in Ṣango's bedroom.

Everything came flashing back. The kisses – had they…? No, she was sure she had stopped him and then…oh, the couch. She remembered with a sigh of relief, much to the amusement of her host.

She gave Ṣango a flustered look. "I'm sorry, I fell asleep on your couch, but you didn't have to —"

"You looked so uncomfortable sleeping on the couch," he said, getting up from the armchair he had been sitting in.

Toyin realised the bedroom had the same interior design as the living room.

"You must like white," she stated, and he smiled at her.

"White and red are my favourite colours. I like my home in white and my women in red," he said, and Toyin grew flustered once more. "Now that you are awake, Órèkelèwá, you should have dinner," he said and gently lifted her off the bed.

"You made dinner?" The question came out more surprised than she had intended.

"Well, technically, you made dinner," Ṣango answered with a smile and carefully led her out of the bedroom and into the dining area. He smelled like oven-baked earth and warm notes, reminding her of the crackling of a bonfire on a starless night. The scent of him proved pleasantly intoxicating, and she wanted to snuggle closer into his body and breathe it all in as he carried her out.

"Wow, you already set the table." She was becoming more and more impressed by the second.

"No small task, I assure you. I had to look through something called Google to figure this all out," he answered as he pulled out a chair and deposited her on it.

"Quite the gentleman, eh." She smiled at him.

"I can be quite charming when I want to," he answered as he took his seat and smiled at her, and she agreed with him because, at this moment, his smile was dangerously charming.

"Eat, Órèkelèwá," he said as she served herself a portion from the casserole.

"Why do you keep calling me that?" She looked at him curiously.

"Because you are incredibly beautiful, and I think it suits you better than Ṣangotoyin. I already know I am mighty enough to be praised; I do not need to be reminded."

Toyin went numb, and her fork fell out of her hands. She was so damn sure she hadn't told him her full name.

Who the hell was this man, and what did he want with her?

CHAPTER SEVEN

"You have a lot of questions. It is understandable. Most humans can barely stand to be in the presence of the divine without losing their wits. You still being in complete hold of your senses is a testament to how strong you are," Ṣango said in all seriousness.

Toyin just couldn't take it anymore.

"You need to stop doing this. People might think you're insane," she warned.

Ṣango smiled and narrowed his eyes at her in a way that made her disconcerted.

"Why are you looking at me like that?" she asked, unable to stop the shiver that ran up her spine.

"It is funny because I thought the same thing of you when you screamed on the stairs the other day. We are quick to judge others insane when we cannot understand the reasons for their actions."

He had a point, but the high-handed way he smiled at her made her roll her eyes at him.

"How do you know my full name? I hardly ever tell anybody because of the judgemental looks I get from people."

Ṣango raised his eyebrows curiously at that statement. "Why would people judge you for your full name? It does not make any sense."

"You should know, your name is Ṣango, so I'm sure you're going through the same thing."

"I can assure you I am not. You still have not told me why your name elicits judgement from other people."

Toyin sighed. She had picked up her fork yet still hadn't been able to eat. The most she'd done with it was stir her food about on the plate. She noticed Ṣango hadn't eaten his food either. Didn't gods eat?

Stop it, Toyin. You cannot start thinking of him as a god. Although he sure as hell looks like one, and he has the weird ability to read thoughts, but... She paused mid-thought because Ṣango was smirking at her.

Damn it. He was reading her mind again.

"Your thoughts wander a lot, do they not, Órèkelèwá?" he asked in a soft, affectionate tone that made her insides melt.

"You seriously need to stop calling me that," she said, but she couldn't hide the flush on her face thanks to her light skin.

To conceal her embarrassment, she cleared her throat and quickly decided to answer his question. All the while, the amusement never left his face.

"It's quite simple, though I never really understood the reasoning behind it. African spirituality is considered evil, especially in Nigeria, where you either have to be Muslim or Christian. If you are anything other than that, you are evil. As a little girl, I learned early not to introduce myself as Ṣangotoyin because I get weird looks from people like I'm a worshipper of the devil or something. By the way, I'm irreligious, so—"

"The Devil," Ṣango repeated.

Toyin could almost swear he shuddered at the name.

"Well, yeah, that's why I don't tell people my full name," she concluded and took a sip of her wine, watching Ṣango through her peripheral vision to see his reaction.

His face devoid of any expression, he simply shrugged.

"Humans are outrageous," he added with a carefree, relaxed look on his face.

Toyin placed her wineglass on the table and looked him straight in the eyes. She wanted answers, and she was going to get them.

"So, what's this whole god business about? How can you read my thoughts? How do you even know my full name? You have to believe me, this is all so weird."

Ṣango leaned back against the dining chair and smiled.

"You will get answers, Órèkelẹ̀wá. That is, after all, why you prepared this exquisite meal."

It was indeed why she had come in the first place, not to apologise. Toyin couldn't help feeling guilty.

Ṣango sat up suddenly, his eyes piercing and profound, and she couldn't look away from them.

"Listen carefully to what I am about to say, for, in my words, you will find the answers to your questions." His voice held a commanding tone that she couldn't refuse. "I am Ṣango, the deity of thunder and fire. I am in the human world to find my Oṣé. I am attached to you because you invoked my wrath upon another human. It was a silly thing to do. Regardless, I am grateful you did because you are one of the few remaining humans who truly believes in the gods. You will help me find my Oṣé, and I will return to the world of the deities."

Toyin's eyes widened in disbelief as she stared at him in utter astonishment for a few seconds after he'd finished talking, and then she sighed.

"I thought you said I would find the answers to my questions in your words. What in all you have just said answers my questions?" The more he spoke, the more disillusioned she became. She simply wanted to smack him across the face for making her more confused.

"I would seriously advise you not to do that."

"Stop reading my thoughts!" God, she was frustrated with him.

"If you will permit me, Toyin, I will explain to you properly what my lord has failed woefully to explain," Gbonka said, surprising both Toyin and Ṣango.

"How did you get here?" she asked when she'd recovered from her surprise. Although she was more than happy to have the handsome man back in the apartment—he seemed a more reasonable person than Ṣango, who needed to have his head checked.

"Through the door, Toyin." He smiled.

"I'm so glad you're back. Can you please explain what is going on to me?" She smiled back at him, highly relieved by his presence. It seemed to ease off the tension in the room somewhat.

Ṣango, on the other hand, did not share her excitement. If anything, he looked displeased at Gbonka's presence.

"I do not seem to recall summoning you back," he said, voicing out the displeasure already evident on his face.

"Forgive me, my Lord, but I have been gone for hours, and I could not keep roaming the streets. People were beginning to give me suspicious looks."

"Why would people suspect you? There is nothing suspicious about you. You are the least suspicious person I know."

"Is he always like this?" Toyin whispered to Gbonka as she eyed Ṣango.

"I hear of the things you do not speak. Do you think I will not be able to hear that which you speak, even if you speak voicelessly?" Ṣango asked her pointedly.

He had a point, but she couldn't help but shake her head at his weirdness. Choosing to ignore him, she pulled Gbonka into a seat at the table.

"Tell me everything," she said, pleading with him for clarity with her big, wide eyes in a way that would be difficult for him to refuse.

"Fine, you try explaining it to her, and let us see if she will understand you. But I promise you there is something wrong with her in the head. What about my words was unclear?" Ṣango mumbled.

Toyin ignored him and looked expectantly at Gbonka.

Gbonka cleared his throat, seemingly enjoying the attention he was getting. "Ṣango's Oṣé is a weapon, a double-headed axe, mighty in the hands of Ṣango, the god of thunder and lightning, one of the most powerful deities in Ìlú Òrìṣà. Nobody else can touch it, much less wield it. No one else is worthy —"

"Hmm, like Thor?" Toyin asked, looking from Gbonka to the still sulking Ṣango.

"What is a Thor?" Ṣango asked, and Gbonka looked equally as confused.

She sighed. "Never mind. Please continue," she said to Gbonka, dead-eyed.

"Anyway, Ṣango fell asleep, and his Oṣé, the symbol of his authority, disappeared."

"I did not fall asleep. I do not sleep," Ṣango protested.

"Of course, my Lord, but the fact remains that you did doze off, and your Oṣé disappeared.

"If you are going to tell the story, tell it right," Ṣango flared. "My Oṣé disappeared because of the ever-conniving Eṣu and that Timi. Oh, I wish I had my Oṣé right now," he added, fuming, and outside, lightning flashed as thunder rumbled.

"Wait, is he doing that?" Toyin looked sharply from one man to the other, but Gbonka's gaze was focused on Ṣango.

"My Lord, please be careful. If you burn down this building out of anger, Olódùmarè will not be pleased, and They really would interfere with your life then," Gbonka cautioned.

The fire in Ṣango's amber eyes subsided.

The craziest thing was that Toyin found she believed them. She shook her head. It had to because her life had been so boring and monotonous, and these men were providing her with entertainment. That had to be the reason. She couldn't actually believe them, could she?

"Wait, Eṣu, as in the devil, and this guy called Timi made your Oṣé disappear?" How much more ridiculous could the story get?

"Eṣu is not the devil. I do not know why humans confuse the two. Eṣu is a sneaky, conniving, sly bastard, and the devil is just..."

There it was. Ṣango shuddered. Toyin had been right—he'd shuddered the first time, too.

"Not even Eṣu himself wants to have dealings with the devil. Please stop talking about him. He is bad luck," Ṣango added.

"Oh, okay." Toyin eyed him. Things were getting weirder and weirder by the minute, but she couldn't deny it proved thrilling listening to their story. Maybe she was also weird.

"To help you understand better, you need to know that Timi is Ṣango's sworn enemy. He became a demi-god because he died full of hatred towards Ṣango. His desire to see Ṣango's end was so strong that it followed him to the afterlife and made him a demi-god. He has been after Ṣango's throne for thousands of years. Their battles are actually a great source of entertainment in Ìlú-Òrìṣà, but Timi Ọlófà-iná keeps losing. Eṣu got bored and decided to rig the games a bit. So, he cast a glamour over the memory of humans, making them doubt the existence of Ṣango. Even his most devout worshippers will doubt his existence, and little by little, they will begin to forget him.

"When a god is forgotten by the humans who worship him, he ceases to be and disappears. The disappearance of Ṣango's Oṣé is a resulting effect of humans forgetting about him. Once he is completely forgotten, he will disappear. But the problem is Eṣu, in his excitement to get some entertainment, forgot that he is one of the most powerful deities and the human mind isn't strong enough to handle his manipulations. Forgetting Ṣango was supposed to be temporary, but it became permanent. The other side effect is that not only Ṣango is being forgotten, but the entire world of the deities is also slipping out of the minds of humans, and our world will completely disappear. The only way to reverse all of this is for Ṣango to get his Oṣé back. The situation is so dire that Oṣun had to make an appearance," Gbonka finally finished.

"You did not have to add that last part, you know that?" Ṣango narrowed his eyes evilly at Gbonka.

"This is a lot to take in." Toyin sighed. "According to stories, isn't Oṣun one of Ṣango's wives?"

Gbonka scoffed. "They are divorced. All three of his wives left him."

"I can see why." She eyed Ṣango. No woman wanted an overbearing man, no matter how handsome he was.

"You are enjoying this, are you not? Having fun at the expense of your lord?" Ṣango kissed his teeth.

"Oh, you are such a whiny baby." Toyin rolled her eyes, and Gbonka stifled a laugh.

Ṣango hissed again. Toyin could tell he wasn't used to being teased, and this somehow made his annoyance cute. She caught herself smiling at him and quickly turned to face Gbonka.

"How do I come into all this? He mentioned something about being attached to me. What does it mean?"

"Well, to revoke the spell and get his Oṣé back, Ṣango must earn the unconditional love of a human. Hatred started all of this; only love can reverse it. We thought it would be difficult to find someone who still believed in Ṣango when you invoked his wrath on another human. To save the world of the deities, we are hoping you would come to love him enough to—" Gbonka paused, making her apprehensive.

"Love him enough to what?" she asked, feeling strongly that she would not like to hear the answer.

"Love me enough to die for me," Ṣango finished the sentence, and she looked at him as if he'd just grown another head.

"Excuse me? Why would I want to do that? Is that why you kissed me? To make me fall in love with you so that you can use me to get your stupid weapon back?" Toyin didn't know where the anger came from, but she was fuming. "Why are men so selfish? My boyfriend wants me to give up my life to nurture his, and you want me to lay my life at your feet so you can live. Not to excuse Ṣeyẹ, but at least I've known him for years. I just met you, and you want me to die for you. What a joke."

She pushed the chair backwards and got to her feet.

"Wait, Toyin, you mis—"

Gbonka tried to say something, but Ṣango stopped him with a slight shake of his head.

"What's so great about you? Who in their right senses would love you enough to die for you?" Toyin snapped at Ṣango, who continued to stare at her stoically. His lack of expression made her even angrier.

"I did," Gbonka said quietly.

But she'd heard him. "You did what?"

"I love Ṣango enough that I died for him, took an arrow straight in my heart in his place."

"Oh, good God." She rolled her eyes. "Then you can die for him again."

"I cannot. If I could, I would have, but I cannot. I am a demi-god now."

"Both of you are crazy. I'm even crazier for sitting here and believing your ridiculous story. What do you think this is? A Percy Jackson novel? Demi-god indeed. And you—" She turned to face Ṣango, still seething. "Thor is a better god because nobody can lift his hammer, much less steal it, and he would never ask anybody to die for him, you stupid freak."

She'd yelled all this at him. Childish, yes, but she was too angry to care. Yet, she detected no change in reaction from Ṣango except a slight twitch of his left eye.

Good, it meant her words had penetrated him at least a little. She turned on her heel and stormed out of their apartment.

CHAPTER EIGHT

"I had no idea she had such a temper on her," Gbonka stated after Toyin had stormed out.

Ṣango knew her words had hurt his friend, but he was doing his best not to show it. He wanted to wring her neck for it. How he had been able to put a leash on his anger was something humans would call a miracle.

"Of course she has a temper. She invoked my wrath on another human out of anger. Even my worshippers do not do that lightly," he said, getting to his feet.

"Why did you not let me correct her misunderstanding?" Gbonka asked.

"It is better that way," he answered simply.

"I do not get you. We are supposed to make Toyin love you. Correcting her misunderstanding would have sped up the process. Fat chance of that happening now."

"Fat chance? You speak like them now." Ṣango shook his head.

"I do not know what you are talking about, but she is our only chance at saving our world. I get it you are a god, and it is natural for you to look disinterested while others do the worrying for you, but this is a serious problem." Gbonka threw his hands up at Ṣango's nonchalance.

"Hmm, this is troubling," he said.

"I am happy you agree with me."

"A person is going around claiming to be me, this Thor person. She says he is more powerful and better-looking. I find that quite disturbing."

Gbonka stared at him open-mouthed. "I do not see how that is an issue right now. It could just be another name you are called in another part of the human world, for all we know. You remember that many stories and legends were created after deities left the human world and language was distorted, all of them varying but ultimately talking about the same thing. She could have been comparing you to you."

"I still do not like it. I cannot be compared to anyone, even another version of myself, as you put it," Ṣango insisted and got to his feet. "We need to find this Thor person."

Gbonka sighed and rubbed his temples. "Fine. At least if you want to find him, Google him first. I heard you can find a lot of people more easily on the internet these days." He then got to his feet and excused himself.

Ṣango watched his friend as he left for his bedroom. He didn't like that Toyin had insulted Gbonka's sacrifice.

He wasn't even the least bothered by this Thor person — it had just been an attempt to make Gbonka forget about the insult, but it hadn't worked. He was going to make Toyin apologise. It was the least he could do.

When he'd found her asleep in an awkward position on the sofa, she'd looked so peaceful. He'd had no idea she had so much venom in her. He should have just let her sleep there and wake up with a kink in her neck instead of carrying her to the bed. It would have served her right.

He strolled to the balcony and gazed at the sky. The human world was so polluted, even stars were disappearing. He shook his head in disgust and disappointment.

His thoughts wondered back to Toyin. What was it about the woman that riled him? None of his wives had the guts she did. Sure, they all hated him. He was short-tempered and arrogant and maybe a little insensitive — at least, those were some of the words they used to describe him. But none of them had ever succeeded in riling him up as much as this Toyin did, and he'd only just met her.

Why would she think he would want her to die for him? One person's death on his conscience proved enough already. She thought too highly of herself, and yet… He scoffed, unable to deny that his heart did flutter a bit when she was around.

He needed to put a leash on his thoughts. Getting her to love him certainly did not involve getting her into his bed, and he'd almost done just that had she not stopped him. It was a risky thing to get into a sexual affair with a human. They always expected too much. It was already complicated enough with deities.

The love he wanted from Toyin was the kind of love Gbonka had for him, a love with no strings attached, unconditional, and without expectations.

Which was why he was afraid. He didn't believe a human like Gbonka existed anymore. They were all selfish, and just his luck to have gotten attached to the most selfish human he'd ever come across. One who was not above hurting others with words.

CHAPTER NINE

Toyin scoffed as she made a list of things she needed to get at the supermarket. She still couldn't believe she had almost fallen for the nonsense Ṣango and Gbonka had spewed earlier.

She had Nollywood to blame for this rubbish. They made her believe madmen roamed the streets in tattered clothes when, in fact, they could be well-dressed, handsome, and even wealthy.

Utter rubbish.

She shook her head and grabbed her purse, slung it across her shoulder, and left for the supermarket. If she was going to take a break from work, she'd rather spend it doing meaningful things, not moping over a selfish ex-boyfriend and a crazy next-door mind-reading neighbour.

Just as she stepped out of her apartment and locked the door, Ṣango came out of his place. His presence took her breath away, and he wasn't even dressed out of the ordinary. He had on black pants, his white shirt unbuttoned at the collar, giving a glimpse of the chain he wore. Something about men who wore necklaces…

The infamous glint in his eyes reminded her she shouldn't be ogling him, and he was the last person she wanted to see, especially after her outburst in his apartment the previous night. She felt a little guilt at the way she had spoken to Gbonka. He was too cute and sweet to be on the receiving end of her anger — she had seen the pain in his eyes when she'd snapped at him. Unlike Ṣango, his heart wasn't made of stone. But she could hardly be blamed when he had practically told her she was to give up her life for a man she barely knew.

Pretending not to see him, she turned and walked towards the stairs.

"Toyin," he called and walked after her.

The urge to answer him proved so strong, yet she kept walking.

"Toyin," he called again, this time more firmly.

Even without turning back to look at him, she could hear the annoyance in his voice.

What did she care? He could get angry and explode into tiny pieces. She kept walking, but just as she was about to start descending the stairs, he grabbed her hand and pulled her to face him.

"I know you heard me, Toyin." His eyes flashed as he spoke through gritted teeth, almost as if it were taking all of his strength to control his anger.

"Ah, ah, are you not a Yoruba man? Don't you know what it means when you call someone, and they don't answer you?" Toyin knew she was walking on a thin line there. He looked utterly dangerous as he glared down at her, yet for some reason, she found it deliciously exciting, and so she matched his glare with her own.

Ṣango scoffed. "Órèkelèwá, you forget that I am a Yoruba god. I do not seem to remember rudeness being a trait of my people."

"Oh, goodness," she breathed. "This is exactly my problem with you. You need to have your head checked. Just because your parents named you after a god doesn't mean you are one. Because you can read minds doesn't make you a god. There are a lot of humans who have that gift, I'm sure. So just stop it." She yanked her hand out of his grip.

To her dismay, Ṣango laughed. "So, that is your problem. You do not believe me. Who do you think you are that I would lie to you?" Still, he didn't seem offended.

"How would I know? I don't know what goes on inside your head."

"Oh, dear Órèkelèwá." Ṣango traced her jawline lightly, almost affectionately. "What am I going to do with you?"

Toyin wanted to purr in his hands like a cat, but she shrugged it off and glared at him stubbornly.

"Look, I have somewhere to be, so if you don't have anything reasonable to say, I'm going."

"Fine, I am going with you."

His earlier annoyance at her had been replaced with a look of amusement.

"Where do you know I'm going, that you want to follow me. Guy better leave me alone."

"You are going to the supermarket, are you not?"

Toyin sighed. She had forgotten he could read minds. "There's no shaking you off, is there?"

"No," he answered, straightforward.

"Fine." She descended the stairs with Ṣango in tow. A car was waiting for them when they got out of the apartment building, and he led her to it.

Toyin didn't know much about cars. This one was black, and with its tinted windows and customised number plate, 'Ṣango,' it all screamed wealth and class, standing out of place in her rough neighbourhood.

Ṣango opened the back door for her and motioned for her to get in. She stared at him open-mouthed for a second. The gesture suddenly made her self-conscious as people stared at her. Her neighbours already didn't like her. That dislike would multiply now that she was getting into an expensive car just as dark and mysterious as its owner.

"What are you waiting for? Get in, Órèkelèwá."

Toyin walked tentatively towards the car, and then she paused and turned sharply towards him, her eyes narrowing in suspicion.

"Wait, are you a yahoo boy? When you say you want me to die for you, it means you want to use me for blood money rituals, abi?"

Ṣango rolled his eyes. "I do not know what a yahoo boy is, and I honestly do not understand the obsession humans have with blood sacrifices. Please, Órèkelèwá, enter the car."

Toyin sighed. It wasn't as if she could refuse when he asked her like that. She got into the car, and he entered close to her then shut the door.

Gbonka sat in the driver's seat and nodded briefly at her, and Toyin felt that pang of guilt hit her again when she remembered how she had spoken to him last night. She had lashed out at both Ṣango and Gbonka, but for some reason, it was only Gbonka she felt apologetic towards.

Ṣango smirked as if he'd read her thoughts, and it hit her that he probably had. She shot him a look, yet his smirk only deepened.

She rolled her eyes and snorted, the smell of the car seat leather and the heady scent of Ṣango's cologne a beautiful combination to her nostrils.

Gbonka started the car, and she had to admit it was a beautiful drive, regardless of the bumpy roads of the area. A ridiculously short drive, as well, because the supermarket was just a few streets away from her house, and she would have trekked had Ṣango not felt the need to show off his wealth.

What was a guy as rich as he was doing in this area of Lagos? Didn't they always prefer to live in Victoria Island or Lekki or Magodo or wherever else rich people lived in this town?

Gbonka pulled into the supermarket's parking lot, and Toyin found she was sad the ride was over.

"Do not worry, we can go for a real ride whenever you want," Ṣango assured her and smiled at her as he held out his hand while she got out of the car.

"Seriously?" she piped up at him, excited, only for her excitement to deflate when she realised he had replied to her thoughts. "This is some serious invasion of privacy. Can't you stop doing that?"

She only got a mysterious smile in response.

"Isn't Gbonka joining us?" she asked as they walked into the supermarket.

"He has some other business to take care of. He will be back just in time to drive us back home."

"Oh." She supposed Ṣango wasn't going to tell her what this business was, and it would be utterly rude of her to ask him.

Shopping with Ṣango turned out to be more fun than she'd expected, if she removed his urge to buy everything expensive even when they did not need it. He was like a child at a candy store, and if she didn't know better, she would have thought it was his first time in a supermarket.

But did she know any better?

He was a man who claimed he was a god, and he wanted her to sacrifice her life for him. He was wealthy, judging by his expensive clothes, the fittings in his apartment, and not to mention his car.

Common sense begged her to stay away from him, yet she couldn't deny she enjoyed being in his company. She felt a pull towards him, an attraction she couldn't resist, and if she wasn't going to kid herself, from the very first time she'd seen him, he'd had an air of divinity around him. Utterly mysterious and endearing. She honestly didn't know what to make of how she felt.

"Come and look at this." Ṣango waved her over.

She smiled and pushed the cart towards where he stood at the stuffed toy section.

"Just look at this. It looks like you." He waved a giant stuffed panda in her face.

"Are you saying I look like a panda?" She stared at him with her mouth slightly agape. Was he trying to call her fat? Should she be offended?

"What's that word you love so much…" He closed his eyes, as if trying to remember. "Cute!" He snapped his fingers as he recalled the word. "It's cute like you and cuddly just like you."

"I'm cuddly?" Toyin laughed.

"Very," Ṣango said and dropped the panda in the cart.

"No way, I already have stuff I don't need because of you."

She took it out, but Ṣango wouldn't have it.

"It is a gift, and I am paying, so let it be." He snatched the animal out of her hands and put it back in the cart.

"I don't need a stuffed panda. I'm not a child, and it's just going to take up space in my apartment."

"You are a cute, cuddly child," Ṣango said, pulling her cheek. "It suits you, so I am giving it to you. You cannot reject a gift from a god."

"Why are you so annoying?" Toyin kissed her teeth and brushed his hand off her cheek.

"Because it ticks you off every time." He smirked.

She opened her mouth to say something, then it occurred to her they were probably creating a scene. So she shut it and shook her head in reluctant submission.

"Toyin?" a familiar voice said, and both she and Ṣango turned to look at who had called.

"Ṣeye," she said in a cold tone. Exactly the person she wasn't ready to see yet.

"Of course, I thought it was you," he said, eyeing Ṣango with suspicion.

CHAPTER TEN

Ṣango didn't need to read Toyin's mind to know who the man standing before them was. The sudden coldness in her demeanour proved all he needed to know of the man's identity, and he didn't like him.

He folded his arms across his chest and fixed his gaze on Ṣeye. The human had an aura about him, similar to someone he knew. Someone he didn't like. But he couldn't jump to conclusions. Many in the human world had the same hateful aura. It was their destiny — they couldn't help it. Also, it was possible he didn't like the man because Toyin had invoked his wrath on him. Only natural that he wouldn't like someone he was supposed to punish.

For now, he would just watch and see what this man wanted with Toyin.

"You haven't been picking my calls or replying to any of my texts," Ṣeye said to Toyin, still side-eyeing Ṣango.

"Is there a reason I should pick your calls? We don't have anything to discuss anymore. We both made ourselves clear." Toyin started to walk past him, but Ṣẹyẹ held her back.

"Are you being serious, Toyin? Can we go somewhere to talk?"

"No, we can't. You didn't come here to talk to me, you accidentally ran into me. So there is no need for you to pretend you care." She yanked her hand out of his grip.

"You are angry. I know you. You are a reasonable woman, and you will soon come to see that our agreement will benefit you. You can't throw all the years we have spent together away like that."

"I don't know what delusion you are living under, but please, can you leave me alone? It is obvious we want different things in life—"

"Think of your mother. Do you think you can take care of her and still go back to school? You need me. You need a man like me—"

At that, Ṣango scoffed, and Ṣẹyẹ looked up at him. They were about the same height, but Ṣango was imposing, and so Ṣẹyẹ found himself looking up at him. Ṣango's grin only deepened.

"Is this why you haven't been picking up my calls? Are you with him now? He looks rich, is that why you are with him? So much for all your Miss Independent attitude." He sneered at Toyin.

Ṣango smiled. There it was. Beneath the handsome likeness, the ugliness that lay under was beginning to rear its head.

"Ahhh, goodness. You know it's not your fault. If Ṣango had done his job and struck you dead like I asked, then you would not stand in front of me to talk nonsense," she hissed and tried to walk past him again, but he pulled her back once more.

Ṣango had had enough. He placed one hand on Ṣẹyẹ's shoulder. His eyes grew dark, his voice low and dangerous — no missing the power in it as he spoke. "Let go of her arm."

Ṣẹyẹ tried to shrug him off, but he couldn't move. He looked into Ṣango's eyes and saw the flash of his amber irises.

"Let go of me, you freak!"

"What is it with humans and name-calling? I am going to say this just once, so listen." As he spoke, the lights in the supermarket went off, and everywhere turned dark while thunder rumbled outside. "You will stay away from Toyin until she is ready to see you and talk to you. You will not bother her again. Otherwise, I will strike you dead like she wants. Do you understand me?"

Ṣẹyẹ was barely able to manage a nod as his whole body shook with fear. His eyes widened in horror, and beads of sweat formed on his forehead and broke into streams running down his face. He tried to speak but couldn't as his face contorted in pain like someone who had a running stomach. Ṣango had only given a glimpse of what it would feel like should he decide to bring down his wrath on him, and his poor soul couldn't even take that little. The pathetic, simpering fool, he was unworthy of Toyin. He shouldn't even be allowed to touch the hem of her garments, and yet this was the man her heart had broken for?

"Good." Ṣango let go of his shoulder.

The lights came back on, and people continued their shopping as if nothing had happened. Of course, for them, nothing had, because time had stopped. The only people who knew what had just taken place were Toyin, who was staring at him awestruck, and Ṣẹyẹ, whose feet had given way underneath him and had fallen to the ground.

"Oh, come on, Órèkelèwá, do not tell me you have fallen for me already." He smirked and pushed the cart to the counter, a dazed Toyin following him like a zombie.

The trip back home was heavy with silence. He found nothing to read in Toyin's mind because it was still frozen, trying to figure out what had happened. The human mind was fragile and could not withhold the might of divinity; that she had not fainted like her boyfriend was a testament to how strong her mind was. But it still didn't stop Gbonka from eyeing him through the side mirror.

Back at the apartment building, he helped her settle into her bedroom and put her to sleep. She would feel better after a nap, and then he turned to face a scowling Gbonka.

"What?"

"You know what. You cannot be flexing your powers in front of humans like that. Why did you not make time stop for her while you did what you did?" Gbonka asked.

"Because I am tired of her disbelieving everything I say. She needs to believe for all of this to work. She will be fine, and so will the other human. He will not be bothering her again, at least for the time being."

"My Lord, I hope you know what you are doing?" Gbonka sighed.

"I always know what I am doing," Ṣango replied.

Gbonka shook his head again.

"What about the thing we discussed this morning?" Ṣango asked, changing the subject.

"I was not able to do a proper check around, given that you messed with the weather, but I will keep looking because I am not comfortable with the aura around."

Ṣango nodded and tapped his friend briefly on the shoulder. "Keep looking. I shall stay here with her until she wakes up. Knowing her, she will have a lot of questions."

"Yes, my Lord." Gbonka bowed and left Toyin's apartment.

Ṣango didn't like the way things were going at all. He wasn't making any progress with Toyin, and then Gbonka had informed him earlier that something was wrong with the atmosphere, yet he couldn't place it.

Deciding not to dwell on questions to which he had no answers, he got up and walked around Toyin's apartment.

How could someone live in such a small space? Her living room, bedroom, and kitchen combined were not as big as one of the rooms in his palace. He didn't even want to think about the bathroom—it was so tiny, it seemed like it had been added to the apartment as an afterthought. He couldn't fit into the toilet without standing sideways.

How could there be room for a bathtub when there was barely any space for a person to stand in it? How in the name of the skies did Toyin take a bath in this tiny excuse of a space?

He shook his head to dismiss the thought. Thinking of Toyin having a bath meant thinking of her naked, and thinking of her naked pushed to the fore the desires he was so desperately trying to fight back. He wanted her legs wrapped around him and her smart mouth moaning his name as he took her to points beyond pleasure. He wanted to cleanse the filth of Ṣẹyẹ off her. But these were dangerous thoughts that could interfere with why he actually needed her, which was why he had to keep himself in check.

Shaking his head, he left the bathroom and went to the kitchen. Toyin would wake up soon, and if she was going to attack him with questions, he might as well feed her because she would need all her strength to fight her own denial.

According to what he'd read from her back at the mall, she was craving chicken pasta. Bringing out his phone, he searched for the perfect chicken pasta recipe and found a video detailing how to make the dish step by step.

He searched through the grocery bags and sorted out the stuff she had gotten before setting to cook the food.

He smiled as a picture of her face when he'd given her the panda formed in his mind. She was so easy to tease, and he immensely enjoyed her company. If that wasn't weird, he didn't know what else was because the only company he ever enjoyed was his own.

CHAPTER ELEVEN

The warm, delicious smell of the food eased Toyin out of her nap. She smiled to herself and hugged her pillow closer. She was craving chicken pasta so much, she was now dreaming of it in her sleep.

Wait… Why was she sleeping? When did she fall asleep?

Her eyes flew open, and she sat up straight in her bed, her brain trying to figure out what exactly had happened.

She had gone to the supermarket to get some groceries. Ṣango had followed her, more like driven her in his exotic car — well, technically, his friend Gbonka had driven her. Then, she'd run into Ṣẹyẹ, and, oh… The memories flooded her: Ṣango's eyes, the darkness that had overcome them.

It had been more seeing Ṣẹyẹ sweat and tremble. Ṣango had looked bigger. She hadn't thought he could look anymore imposing than he already did, but in that moment, he *had* looked bigger and dazzling, wrapped in a magnificent shroud of fire, his eyes dark and fiery at the same time. The fire around him had called to her. As a child, she'd learned not to play with fire, yet this fire, she wanted it to embrace her, to consume her. It drew her in, and then just before she could step into it, the lights had come back on as suddenly as they had gone out, and everyone and everything had returned to normal. It seemed not even Ṣẹyẹ with whatever Ṣango had done to him had witnessed what she had. It was a memory she could never erase. A feeling she could never forget.

Ṣango was more than a mind-reading psychic. He was indeed a deity. The acceptance of this unlikely truth sent tingles to her toes.

She got out of bed and followed the delicious smell to her kitchen, where Ṣango was cooking. He had his sleeves rolled up and looked serious as he turned the spaghetti in the pot. She didn't think he could look any sexier than this.

Focus, Toyin, you have a divine being who's only supposed to exist in the myths cooking in your kitchen. The last thing you should be thinking of is how sexy he looks.

"I felt you wake up," Ṣango said without looking up at her.

"You really are a deity," she blurted out and immediately regretted it. Memories of how rude she had been to him in the past few days came back at her. She had even compared him to Thor. She just wanted the ground to open up and swallow her. If there was anything the myths had taught her, it was that deities were jealous beings, and she'd gone ahead and —

Ṣango smirked and looked up at her. He'd heard all the things she had just thought, and he was laughing at her. *Laughter is good.* It meant he wasn't angry, or was this the laughter before he brought down the thunder and fire on her?

This time, he did laugh out loud.

"You are hungry, and I have noticed you have no table to set, so I'll just —"

"I'll bring the plates," she said and cleared her throat as she brushed past him to get the crockery from the cabinets. Given how small her kitchen was, the contact proved unavoidable, and it set off tiny sparks all over her body.

She froze.

Was this it? Was this the beginning of Ṣango's fire that would eventually consume her entire being?

"Stop it, Toyin." The words were a command, but he sounded more amused than angry. Although his voice stayed low, there was no hint of contempt in the way he looked at her. Instead, his eyes were dark, as dark as they had been in his apartment when he had planted delicate yet fiery kisses all over her body.

He pulled her close her to him with one arm, the other resting against the kitchen counter for support. She relaxed her full weight against him and looked him in the eyes, sure the lust there must be a reflection of hers.

"Órèkelèwá, I am a god, not a demon. I do not go about killing people."

Drawing her closer as if she weren't already pressed tightly against him, he brought his mouth to meet hers. The force of the contact made her gasp in surprise. He took advantage of the opening and let his tongue explore her mouth.

Time stopped.

She had never been devoured like this before. Ṣẹyẹ's kisses didn't even come close, and even the little nibbles Ṣango had planted all over her body were nothing compared to what his mouth and tongue were doing to her now. She wanted more. So, she gave herself to him as their tongues engaged in a slow, passionate dance.

She felt every bit and inch of him against her. Proof he wanted her as much as she wanted him. Her hands explored the hardness of his chest, and just as she began to unbutton his shirt, he pulled away.

Both of them breathing heavily, he moved from her and walked out of the apartment.

First came the stunned confusion and then the realisation of what had almost happened. Next came the overwhelming feeling of shame.

Toyin wanted to die.

What was wrong with her? This was the second time she had thrown herself at him in the little while she had known him. Well, strictly speaking, he had initiated it both times, but the way her body had reacted to him each time was unlike her and maybe even unnatural.

Ṣango was the last person she should be doing this with. He wasn't even human, for goodness' sake. She was just a human he probably wanted to toy with until he went back to wherever he came from, and she was making it easy for him.

This wasn't her. She was never overly sexual. In her relationship with Ṣẹyẹ, sex was something she'd only done because it was expected in a relationship. She'd never really liked it or hated it, but here she was throwing herself at a deity.

That explained it!

Ṣango was a god. He probably exuded some divine erotic magnetic aura that, as a human, she wasn't immune to. It had to be the only reason she was behaving like this.

Toyin sighed as she looked at the once enticing food in the pot that had never made it to her plate. He'd even gone through the trouble of cooking for her, and now, she had no appetite.

She left the kitchen and sat dejectedly on the sofa in her living room. Maybe she should go and explain to him. Then again, what was she going to tell him? It would be better to avoid him. Yet, how was it possible to avoid him when according to him, she was the reason he was here.

It was all so confusing, she felt as if she were losing her mind. She sighed again and caught sight of the panda Ṣango had bought for her. How had she missed it before? So giant, it had taken more than half the living room.

The answer was simple. The one who had bought it was literally and figuratively larger than life, and he had been in her apartment. So of course, there was no way she would have noticed anything else.

She crawled to where the panda sat and wrapped up against it. It was oddly and strangely comforting. Ṣango had been right; it was cuddly, and maybe that's why — or maybe there was another reason she couldn't quite point out — she found herself sobbing into the stuffed bear.

How infuriating: she didn't know why she was crying. *Bullshit.* She knew why she was tearing up. Everything was so overwhelming. She hadn't fully come to terms with her breakup when suddenly, a god appeared in her life to tell her his fate and the fate of the world lay in her willingness to love and die for him.

Why did she have to die? Why was her body betraying her? Why did she have to curse Ṣẹyẹ at that moment? What was so special about her? Why did she have so many questions?

It was just too much for her.

She hugged her panda and cried, too absorbed in her sadness to notice that Ṣango had materialised into her apartment and was standing in a corner watching her intently.

CHAPTER TWELVE

"We need to find someone else," Ṣango declared.

Gbonka, who was browsing through TV channels in their shared apartment, looked at him with one eyebrow raised. "I do not understand what you mean, my Lord."

"Toyin. I do not think she is strong enough to handle the magnitude of the weight that has been placed on her shoulders." He stopped pacing to sit beside Gbonka.

"You know how lucky we were to find someone who still slightly believes you are real. The world thinks you are a myth. Even if there is a chance someone still believes in you in a world filled with billions of people, you are tethered to her, and she to you. The only person who can break it off is the one who created the connection in the first place. If by any chance, you are willing to see your ex-wife again, then by all means do."

Although he didn't particularly care for Gbonka's tone, his friend was right. It would be foolish to break off the connection and then wander the human realm to find another person who still partially believed in his existence. That would take the entire duration of the time he had to spend on Earth, and to break the connection, he had to deal with Ọṣun, and he didn't want to.

"Are you for some reason angry with me?"

"My Lord, I am not worthy enough to be angry with you," Gbonka replied, but he wouldn't take his eyes off the television.

He was definitely angry.

"You are, and I would like to know why." When Gbonka did not answer, he added, "That is an order."

Gbonka sighed and dropped the remote, then turned to face him. "Why, can I not be angry in peace? You just had to order me to tell you why I am angry, Ṣango."

Ṣango raised an eyebrow, a bit taken aback by Gbonka's fierceness. Gbonka had only once been seriously angry with him, and that had been millennia ago.

"Is the human world rubbing their insolence off on you? Why are you speaking to me like that?"

Gbonka closed his eyes and took a deep breath. "Permit me to speak freely."

"You are already speaking freely," Ṣango pointed out.

"Did you take her to your bed?" Gbonka blurted out.

"Who? Did I perhaps take a woman of yours to bed before we came here?"

"Do not play dumb. You know who I am talking about. But let us pretend you do not know what I am talking about. I shall clarify. Did you take Toyin to your bed?"

Ṣango stared at him blankly for a few seconds, and then a mischievous grin spread across his face.

"Stop grinning like the Cheshire cat and answer the question."

"Why are you calling me a cat?" Ṣango asked, genuinely offended, and his friend rolled his eyes.

"It would do you a little good to familiarise yourself with earthly literature while you are here."

"Literature, books." Ṣango scoffed and shuddered.

"Do not try to change the subject and answer the question."

"What is it to you? Do you want her?"

"She is not an object. I cannot want her, and I already have a woman waiting for me back at home, and unlike you, I can stay faithful to one woman for the rest of eternity," Gbonka said.

Ṣango narrowed his eyes calmly at his friend, getting tired of the conversation. He wasn't one to talk too much, and that's all he'd been doing since he got to the human world.

"What are you driving at?"

"You are acting strange, and I have only seen you act this way once, when you first met your third wife."

"What are you talking about?" Ṣango sat up, his interest awakened at the mention of Ọya.

"You know exactly what I am talking about. Just remember, before you mess things up, what is at stake. Your life, mine, the entire world of deities and the entirety of the human world. If the majority of humans do not start believing in the existence of the deities again, then we are all going to perish."

"I already know all of that, so what—"

"I am telling you to focus!"

"Gbonka!"

"Stop trying to get her to sleep with you and start trying to get her to like you. Otherwise, we will not be able to break Eṣu's curse."

"Gbonka, I understand, but you may stop speaking freely now."

"Yes, my Lord," Gbonka said and gave a stiff bow as he got up to his feet, obviously happy to have passed across his point.

"Wait," Ṣango called him back.

"My Lord."

"To be honest with you, I am not getting anywhere with Toyin. I find myself attracted to her in ways that I cannot control, and if I am to earn her devout love, I cannot allow myself to give in to my desires. My presence in her life seems to hurt her. I hate to say this, but I do not know what to do," he admitted.

Gbonka sighed and came back to sit on the sofa he'd just vacated.

"Apart from the gift of eternal life and all that comes with it, the women of the human world are not much different from the women in the world of deities. What they want is a friend who listens to them and treats them wholesomely. Instead of asserting your will over her as a deity, it would do well for you to just be her friend. We may not be able to understand it, but this whole situation is a lot for her to bear, and let us not forget that she has her own human problems, too."

"You are telling me to dial down my authority and come down to her level?"

"No, I am saying you should treat her the way you would treat a goddess because, let us face it, no matter how powerful you are, a god, you would never mistreat a goddess and get away with it," Gbonka concluded.

The more Ṣango thought about it, the more it made sense. He had popped up into her life and had basically been harassing her since, following her everywhere, invading her thoughts and her privacy.

He was pressed for time. It would be good for her to love him now so he could return to where he belonged and put an end to Timi and his nonsense, but it would be unfair for him to put pressure on Toyin.

When did he start caring about other people's problems? This was Toyin's fault. She was changing him in ways he didn't understand, and he needed to figure out his thoughts.

It would be better to take several steps away from her and leave her alone to sort out her emotions.

He looked at his friend, and although he tried not to show it, Gbonka was on edge. He was a warrior, not someone who should be locked up in a tiny apartment. He should be on the field training his soldiers. He should be back home with his woman. Ṣango understood why he'd been angry earlier. Taking Toyin to his bed could severely hinder her chances of loving him, and then, they may not be able to go back home.

This mission had been simple enough when Ọṣun had explained it. Nobody had expected Toyin to be such a strong-willed woman and for him to be so emotional and tactless.

He needed a nap. He hadn't slept since they'd arrived in the human world, partly because he didn't need to sleep and also because, after the disappearance of his Oṣé, he'd been wary of anything that would make him lose consciousness. But now, he could use the nap, and maybe when he woke up, he would be able to navigate his mind and feelings better.

He lay back against the couch and closed his eyes. Five minutes later when he opened them, it was with renewed determination to do things right.

CHAPTER THIRTEEN

Toyin had cried herself to sleep hugging the panda, and when she opened her eyes, it was a little past midnight. Still, it felt as if both the tears and the rest had helped her see clearly.

The truth she was now admitting to herself was that she liked Ṣango. Nothing as deep as love or whatever it was he wanted from her. She had loved only one man all her life, and it had ended badly.

Ṣango was a deity, which still proved a bit difficult for her to wrap her mind around, yet it was the truth. As a deity, he would be able to understand her and the reasons for her actions.

Getting to her feet, she brushed down her clothes in a futile attempt to remove the creases lying on the cold, hard-tiled floor had created on them. Without thinking or looking at the time, she would go see Ṣango and tell him her mind. They needed to talk out whatever it was between them.

Opening her door, she was surprised to find Ṣango standing just outside it, about to knock.

"Oh," she mouthed in surprise. "I was just about to come and see you."

He nodded, a slight smile playing across his lips.

"We need to talk," they both said at the same time.

Toyin gave a short awkward laugh and straightened up. She had to keep her wits about her if she wanted to have a full and meaningful conversation with Ṣango. And given the sparks between them, they couldn't have said conversation in an enclosed space if she wanted to achieve that.

"Do you mind if we go to the roof?" she asked him, and he nodded in agreement.

"It is the only place in this building that I like," he admitted as they walked to the stairwell that led up to the roof.

For a six-storey building, it proved a huge inconvenience that the structure didn't have an elevator. Yet, none of the tenants complained because it was of no use — the building was old, and the agent didn't care whether or not it was in good condition or convenient enough for the tenants. The tenants, on their part, were grateful to at least have running water. Epileptic electricity was a nationwide problem, so nobody cared about that. All in all, it was a good place for the amount of rent they paid.

"You have been to the roof?"

"The apartment is a bit too confining for me. I love open spaces. My palace…" Ṣango trailed off.

No doubt he was taking her into consideration as she was still getting used to him being a deity and all.

"I would love to know more about your world, your palace," Toyin said, prompting him on. She needed him to keep talking. Either that, or they would have to climb the stairs in awkward silence, during which she might lose her resolve to speak to him openly and plainly.

"Oh, I would not know where to start, describing the world of the deities," Ṣango said, yet, the tone of his voice told her he would be more than happy telling her all about it.

"You can start anywhere." He had piqued her interest with his desire to talk about his world.

"One of the most beautiful things about Ìlú Òrìṣà is the greenery. Compared to this world, the world of deities is fresher, cleaner, more breathable. The trees and plants are alive—"

"Trees and plants are alive here, too," she interrupted.

"No. Here, they are living. In Ìlú Òrìṣà, they are alive. There is a difference. One could have a conversation with them, and they have personalities and feelings," he explained.

Toyin paused to look at him, a look he probably mistook to be one of disbelief.

"If you find it difficult to believe this minor detail, then you will not be able to believe anything else I have to tell you because, trust me, there is a lot to tell you." He laughed.

As a child, she'd loved stories, reading them, listening to them, and even telling them. If she had to choose something else aside from becoming a neurosurgeon, she would have become a storyteller. She felt a rush of excitement in her veins at the stories Ṣango would tell her.

"I believe you. I just think it's cool to be able to talk to a tree or a flower and have them respond to you."

Ṣango laughed at that. "Though, I must tell you they are proud creatures. They know how important their existence is to the world, and they do not fail to rub it in our faces."

Toyin smiled and continued climbing, only to miss a step and fall backwards. Ṣango immediately caught her, his palm supporting the small of her back to prevent her from falling. An unintentional yet intimate gesture that reminded her of the first time she'd met him.

Ṣango cleared his throat and let her go once her footing was secure. She glanced away and rushed her ascent up the stairs. The sooner they got this conversation over with, the better for her.

The roof was refreshingly cool. There were benches where they could sit, but cooped up in their apartments all day, they decided to stand.

She smiled as he lifted his face towards the sky and took in a deep breath.

"You must miss home."

He turned to look at her and smiled. "Hm, I do. Not that I cannot go back if I wanted to, but of what use is returning home without my Oṣé, the reason I came here in the first place."

Toyin thought about how nice it must be to have such a place to return to, where trees had personalities and spoke. She wanted to know more about his world, and she maybe would even like to see it.

That was wishful thinking. She had to focus on what was possible.

"You said you had something to say to me," she blurted out. Better if they went straight to the point, to know where they both stood with each other.

"I think I would rather hear what you have to say to me first," Ṣango replied.

She noticed not for the first time since he'd shown up at her door that his tone was gentle and a little less commanding than ordinarily.

"As if you don't already know what I want to tell you." She scoffed.

"Ah, that." He laughed. "I have stopped reading your thoughts. Looking into the minds of humans is nothing out of the ordinary for me. But you find it intrusive, and if I am to be your friend, I would have to stop doing that."

Toyin looked at him disbelievingly and then laughed. "I had no idea you had it in you to be considerate of other people."

"Not other people. Even as a deity, it is beyond my ability to be considerate of other people. But people I consider my friend, I would do all within my power to make them comfortable."

She liked this side of him. Only Ṣango could perfectly balance being insufferable and amiable at the same time. But how was she supposed to say all she had to say to him if he was this sweet and considerate?

"Would you like to be my friend?"

His voice was soft and gentle. Looking into his eyes, she saw his intense sincerity.

She took a deep breath and let it out slowly. She had to do this — she needed to speak out her mind now for herself.

"I know I'll never be able to grasp or even understand how important going back home is for you, but Ṣango, I cannot die for you. I'm not even sure I am capable of loving anyone apart from myself at this moment, much less loving someone enough to die for him." She paused, watching his reaction to what she had just told him, and she wasn't sure what she saw in his amber eyes.

Feeling the need to explain further and because of the heaviness of his silence, she continued.

"I have to choose myself for the first time in my life. I have dreams, dreams I am closer to achieving now than I have ever been before. I am an only child. My parents couldn't have any children after they had me. My father was murdered when I was ten by armed robbers. He was hacked in the head by their machetes. He made it to the hospital, and he could have survived, but there was no neurosurgeon at the hospital. He had to be transferred to a bigger health centre, but he didn't make it there. He died in the ambulance transferring him to the hospital. My mother's health isn't doing too well either, and she lives back in my hometown. The only way I can properly take care of her is to go after my dreams and to succeed at them. This means I cannot afford to die now. It is why I cannot love you because loving you means I have to die."

She finally finished talking and had to catch her breath. She hadn't realised that while she had been pouring her heart out, she had been holding her breath.

In all of this, Ṣango had remained quiet, watching her intently. She looked at him, blinking expectantly, waiting for him to reply.

"Well, say something…"

Instead of talking, he pulled her into a tight hug. The gesture took her by surprise, yet she found herself melting into his embrace. This wasn't how it was supposed to go. This wasn't where the discussion was supposed to lead. So why did she find his embrace so comforting and warm?

"It was not my desire to place such a burden on you, Órèkelèwá," he said into her ear. "I have been unfair, and I admit my faults since we are being completely honest with each other. When I came here, this mission was simply to get you to love me. After all, how possible is it for a human to resist loving a deity? The truth is I had not expected to grow so fond of you, so much that I am willing to find someone else who might slightly remember me to lift this burden off you. Unfortunately, that is not possible to find. You must have misunderstood the kind I love I want from you, but it is not something I can explain to you. It is something you would have to discover for yourself."

Ṣango pulled away from her but still kept his hand around her waist as he looked deeply into her eyes.

"Órèkelèwá, I want to spoil and pamper you. As a deity, I am not allowed to interfere freely in the destiny of humans. Even the god of destiny does not have that privilege. Otherwise, it would not take me more than a second to lift all the burdens in your life. Regardless, I would like you to give me a chance to make it a little less hard for you."

Toyin blinked twice. She wasn't sure she'd heard Ṣango correctly. She had just told him she couldn't give him what he wanted from her, and instead of getting angry or trying to persuade her, he was offering her respite. What was she to make of this?

How seriously should she take his words?

"Give me a chance to treat you like a goddess," Ṣango added. His voice was still soft and soothing and honestly very tempting.

Toyin was sure of how she felt and what she wanted in her life, but this gorgeous man—no, deity—was pleading with her to reconsider and not be totally close-minded.

She was just an ordinary human. There was nothing special about her that Ṣango would ask this of her. She couldn't help him find his weapon, and it only made sense that he should leave to find a person who could help him. She wasn't a hero.

But in truth, did she want him to disappear from her life? She knew the answer to the question, which was why even though common sense was against her response, she took a deep breath.

"I would very much like to be treated like a goddess. What woman wouldn't want to? However, if we are going to be friends, there are going to be rules."

"Rules?" Ṣango repeated with a raised eyebrow, and his infamous grin spread across his face.

"Yes. Rules." She looked at him with nothing but sheer determination.

CHAPTER FOURTEEN

"You cannot possibly be serious," Ṣango blurted out in utter dismay.

They had left the roof and were now in his pristine apartment, where they had spent the better part of the night drafting Toyin's ridiculous set of rules for their friendship. Neither of them had noticed the sun was already coming up until the light started peeking through the curtains.

"I'm dead serious." She looked at him without blinking.

"What do you mean, no touching?"

"It means exactly what it means. No touching of any kind, no kissing, no hugging, nothing whatsoever," she explained.

"How can we be friends if I cannot touch you? How does that make sense?"

"You don't have to touch me for us to be friends. Besides, weird things happen when we touch each other," she explained and went back to the list she was writing.

"By weird things, do you mean the fire that burns through your body begging for me to quench it, or is it the one you want to overcome you?" He grinned mischievously.

Toyin stared at him for a few seconds, blinked twice, and then bent to put down another rule in the journal she was using.

"What... What are you writing now?"

"No smirking, grinning, or looking devilishly or mischievously handsome."

"Ah!" he exclaimed.

"What is *Ah*? Do you want this to work or not?" She stared at him stoically, but she was enjoying his dismay. "And, no mind-reading," she said as she wrote it down.

"We already agreed on that," he said, rolling his eyes.

"I know, but it is important to write it down to avoid any misunderstanding in future."

He snatched the notepad out of her hands and went through the list of rules she had written.

No walking around shirtless
Respect boundaries
No demand for sacrifices
No touching whatsoever
No smirking, grinning, or looking devilishly sexy
No mind-reading

Ṣango scoffed at the ridiculousness of the rules. If the other deities heard what he was doing for a human woman, he would never be able to live it down. Still, he couldn't deny the warmth brewing within him as he read the list, or maybe it came from the excitement vibrating in Toyin's body. She wanted to be his friend as much as he wanted to be hers.

"Would you like to make your own list of rules?"

She seemed to be holding her breath as she stared at him expectantly.

He laughed at that. The rules were for her protection; he understood that much. Rules were made by those who had something to lose. He was immortal, and when he found his Oṣé, he would return to his world, and she would be left behind to deal with the aftermath of whatever their relationship was about to become.

He smiled and moved to stroke her beautiful face, then he remembered the no-touching rule and put his hand down. He sighed. The no-touching rule was going to be the most difficult of all.

Then an idea struck him, and his grin broadened. "I have only one rule."

She perked up, blinking at him excitedly.

"What is it?" she asked when he only looked at her smiling.

"When I call you, you must answer. No matter what."

She sighed, a bit disappointed. "You just can't relinquish control, can you?" She laughed.

"What, I did not argue with any of your rules, so you cannot contend with mine?"

"You argued all through this list, and might I remind you that this list will only continue to grow as time goes by."

"Whatever." He rolled his eyes.

"Ohhh, look at you adapting to our earthly lingo."

She poked at him, and Ṣango couldn't help the smile that spread across his face.

"Where's Gbonka?" she asked, looking around the apartment for any signs of his friend. "I haven't seen him around since we got back from the supermarket. Is he avoiding me?"

"Is there a reason why he would be avoiding you?" Ṣango asked, his voice taking up a serious tone. He'd meant to talk to her about her outburst the other day, but so many things kept coming up, he'd forgotten to discuss it with her.

"I want to apologise for the way I lashed out at him the other day. I tend to say stupid things when I get angry," she admitted, shamefaced, as if he needed a reminder. She had invoked his wrath on a person in the fit of anger.

Ṣango smiled. Now that he wasn't reading her thoughts, it was difficult to put together what was going on in her head, but he was happy she had decided to apologise for what she had done.

"Gbonka is on an assignment. We will not be seeing him until he completes it," he answered.

"You won't tell me what the assignment is?"

He shook his head. He couldn't discuss what it was with her until they figured it out.

Something dangerous was lurking around. Its heaviness hung in the air like a bad smell, but they couldn't quite tell what it was. So after their talk, he'd sent Gbonka out to investigate what it might be.

Yet, he couldn't tell Toyin all of that. He didn't want to scare her with the thought of evil lurking around. She might be a strong-willed human, but the events of the past few days had proven to him that no matter how strong she was, she was still human, and there was a limit to what her mind could bear.

"Now that we have the rules all sorted out, what do we do now?" she asked him.

He could think of a million things he wanted to do to her, but he would keep to the rules and let her take charge.

"Whatever you want, Órèkelèwá. Whatever you want."

CHAPTER FIFTEEN

"Whatever you want, Órèkelẹ̀wá. Whatever you want."

They were just words, yet why did they sound so sexy coming from his mouth? Toyin shook her head to dispel the thoughts. She'd made the rules, and she was going to stick by them.

"Are you alright?" Ṣango asked, seeing her shake her head, a playful grin spread across his face. He was doing this intentionally, but she wouldn't give him a chance.

"Wow, look at the time. We talked through the night, so for now, I think we both need to sleep."

"I do not sleep," he said, straightforward. "But judging by the bags and dark circles around your eyes, you do need to sleep."

She rolled her eyes and got to her feet, yawning as a wave of tiredness suddenly hit her.

"No one's ever told you not to tell a woman she has bags under her eyes?" she asked, not really expecting an answer as she walked towards the door.

He followed behind her, and she turned to smile at him.

"To our first day as friends." She stretched her hand forward for a shake, but Ṣango only stared at her with a blank expression on his face. "When someone does this, it means they want you to shake their hand. It is a sign of friendship or —"

"I know what it means," he cut her off abruptly. "But you made the no-touching rule, not me."

Toyin sighed. She had temporarily forgotten who she was dealing with. Shaking her head, she left his apartment and made for hers. Once in, she collapsed on her bed and fell asleep almost immediately.

She woke up to the sound of someone knocking on her door. She got out of bed and groggily walked that way and opened it. Her eyes flew open, and the remnants of sleep disappeared from her perception when she saw Ṣango standing on the landing.

How awful she must look with her eyes swollen from sleep and her hair dishevelled, and she was still in the clothes she had worn to the mall. What would it have cost her to have taken a little care before opening the door?

"Since when did you start knocking?" she asked, attempting humour to divert his attention from the way she looked.

"We must respect each other's boundaries, remember?" he answered as he casually stepped into her apartment.

"You don't have to keep referring to the list every time we see each other. You can just follow them." She shut the door and sidestepped his imposing frame to come face him. "What are you doing here, anyway?"

She tried to seem uninterested that he was in her apartment when all she wanted to do was dash into the bathroom to freshen up and look a little bit presentable. How she always managed to appear so scrappy beside him was beyond her. He always looked so effortlessly sexy.

"I needed to check if you were still alive. You've been asleep for hours," he answered, plopping himself on her couch.

Toyin looked at the time — quarter past seven in the evening, and she'd gone to sleep just as the sun was rising. She couldn't believe she had slept for that long. He was right to check up on her, but why was he lounging on her sofa? He should leave. She needed to clean up and maintain her dignity.

"You have a little something here," he said, touching his cheek.

Her hand slowly went to her right cheek, where her worst fears were realised. Dried saliva. Her eyes widened in horror, and she rushed into the bathroom, but not before she saw the smile creeping up Ṣango's face.

What could be more embarrassing than the man you were pretending not to like seeing in you in your worst physical state? Worse, it wasn't the first time—she remembered how she had looked when they'd first met on the staircase, and it made her want to bury her head in the toilet bowl.

Thirty minutes later, she returned to the living room, freshly showered and in clean pyjamas, a bonnet covering her head. Her natural hair had matted from the lack of care she had given in the past few days, and it would not only take time to get back into order, it would also give her a headache. The best option had been to cover it up with a silk bonnet.

Stepping out of the bathroom, her first instinct had been to put on some makeup and wear her Sunday best, yet it would have been obvious she was trying hard. They were supposed to be friends, and friends wore their pyjamas around each other all the time, didn't they?

He was scrolling through his phone when she came back into the living room, and he looked up at her, giving her a once-over before breaking into his infamous mischievous grin.

What, now?

"Darling, you need to go back inside and change into something else," he said.

"Why would I do that?" she asked, sitting on the floor and folding her legs into an easy yoga pose.

"Because we are going out," he declared, like they had discussed it before.

"Going out where? And at this time? Abeg, me, I'm not going anywhere o."

"Gbonka said the nightlife in this city is beautiful. I would like to see it, and you are coming with me." His amber eyes glowed as he spoke.

"But I don't want to go outside."

"You have no choice." Ṣango got to his feet. "When I call, you must answer. That is my only rule, remember," he said as he hurled her to her feet and pushed her towards her bedroom.

Toyin reluctantly let him push her inside. She indeed did not have a choice. Quickly pulling out a pair of jeans and a black tee, she was soon good to go and about to step out of her bedroom when she remembered the bonnet on her head. She sighed and sat at her messy vanity, spraying some water and rubbing in the leave-in-conditioner. She worked as fast as she could through her hair, grateful it had decided to cooperate with her that evening. One would think all the struggle would amount to an elegant hairstyle when all she wanted to do was just put her hair into a bun.

Her hair was full, thick, and typical 4c strands, which meant it required a lot of care and attention. With all that had been going on lately, she'd barely had the time to care for it. She'd been contemplating cutting it, but she wasn't sure she had the heart to cut her beautiful hair that, when straightened, hung just a few inches from her waist. It was worth the struggle.

Finally succeeding in pulling it into a bun, she added some edge control gel to get perfect baby hair edges and then dabbed a bit of powder on her nose and cheekbones and a little lip gloss to her lips, deciding to go without earrings.

Looking at herself in her mirror, satisfied with the results, she stepped out to where Ṣango was patiently waiting.

"For someone who does not want to go out, you sure took your time in getting dressed," he said.

Still, the glint in his eyes meant he was pleased. She rolled her eyes at him. With all the time he had on his hands, one would think he would take some of that time to care for his hair, but he only used his time to pester her. He was due for new braids. Though, the rough look suited him. She doubted there was anything he didn't look good in. She would love to get her hands in his hair and work some magic. She could already imagine the feel of his thick curls through her fingers.

"Yeah, yeah, whatever. Let's go," she replied haughtily, though her stomach tightened with excitement when they left the apartment.

CHAPTER SIXTEEN

Toyin had no idea how beautiful she was. Even when dishevelled, her beauty still overshadowed whatever state she might be in. Ṣango was in way over his head with this whole friendship thing, and he knew it. He wanted more time with Toyin to ease her worries; he wanted his shoulder to be the one she leaned on, his shirt the one to soak her tears, and his words those to bring a smile to her face.

But it wasn't possible to abandon his destiny. He had his duties to uphold as a deity. If he left those, then he might as well damn himself to Àjalè èsín — the dungeon of disgrace.

He had seen deities fall in love with humans, and he'd wondered why anyone would want to put themselves in such a difficult situation. He'd never once imagined he could find himself in such a predicament. Yet, here he was, about to risk it all for this one human. He had fallen in love only once, and that had ended badly. He wasn't going to put himself through all of it again.

He also hadn't been able to reach Gbonka since he'd gone on the assignment. He couldn't feel their connection, the one they'd had since his friend had lain down his life for him.

Gbonka was a warrior, strong and smart enough to make his way about, but Ṣango still couldn't help being worried about him. He wanted to see the city with Toyin, and it was also an opportunity to search around for Gbonka or feel the connection with his spirit at least once again so he could be at ease.

"Are we not going in your car?" Toyin asked as they stepped out of the apartment building, the smell of sewage and exhausts assaulting their noses as they did.

"Gbonka left with the car," he answered, leading her towards the bus stop.

"So, how are we going to get around?"

"You'll see," he said, smirking as he hailed a Keke coming their way.

"Oh, you're a natural at this. Where did you learn how to do that?" she asked him.

He only shrugged as they entered the tricycle.

"Suya Junction," he said to the rider, and the man zoomed off.

"Suya Junction?" Toyin asked, the disbelief in her voice clear. "How do you know Suya Junction?"

"Just relax and enjoy the evening with me, will you? And close your mouth. Otherwise, a fly might enter it," he said and smirked when she shut her mouth abruptly.

They could smell the delicious aroma of the peppered barbecued beef as they drew closer to Suya Junction, and Toyin's stomach rumbled. She clutched her belly in embarrassment; Ṣango pretended not to hear it.

The driver parked at the famous Suya Junction. As usual, it was packed with people at that time of the day. Various stands stood around, under the cover the darkness and the aroma of the charcoal, the smoke from the fire sizzling beef, and the smell of raw onions.

They took one look at the queue, and when Toyin's stomach growled again, she flushed. This time, Ṣango couldn't help the grin that spread across his face.

"It's not like I'm really hungry like that. I'm just reacting to all the smoke and the—"

"Yeah, really, maybe we should just turn back and go somewhere else, then?" He smirked and turned as if leaving, and Toyin grabbed his hand.

"We're already here, and it would be such a waste to leave," she said, clearing her throat to hide her embarrassment.

"No touching." He snatched his hand, although not in an aggressive way. He couldn't help the grin across his face as Toyin moved to join one of the long queues.

He knew she hadn't eaten anything in two days, and he didn't want to have to cook for her again, given how it had turned out the last time. She needed to take better care of herself, but it seemed like she couldn't be bothered with it. So, until he had to leave, he would take it upon himself to take care of her.

Ṣango looked around the crowd. It wouldn't do—he'd never had to wait for anything in his entire life, and he didn't intend to start now.

"Do you want to feel like a queen?" he whispered in Toyin's ear after bending to her, and smiled when she looked at him, confused.

His amber eyes glowed as he stood up straight, and his smirk deepened as he snapped his fingers. It took Toyin a few moments, then he saw the glint in her eyes when she realised what he had done.

The smile spreading across her face as the crowd parted for them to pass made him utterly satisfied. Walking proudly amidst the packed crowd of people who for the moment had no control over their senses, like a queen who was about to address her subjects, confirmed she was made for the luxurious life. She just didn't know it.

When they got to the Suya vendor, he released the hold over the crowd's minds. They had no idea how time had stopped for them. None of them was strong-willed enough to resist the hold of his power over their minds.

Toyin placed their order, and while the vendor prepared their meat, she used the toothpick provided to check the samples of barbecued beef that had been cut out on the table, picking up a piece to then dip it into the sauce. Ṣango watched how she put it into her mouth and closed her eyes as she savoured the taste. He enjoyed watching the look of pure ecstasy on her face.

"I've missed this," she said. "I can't believe it. I live so close to Suya Junction, and I haven't been here in a long time."

Ṣango smiled at her. He enjoyed how she was enjoying herself. He hadn't sensed Gbonka so far since he had stepped out, but he was happy just looking at Toyin.

"Oga, don't put plenty onions o," she said to the vendor as she dipped another piece into the sauce. This time, she brought it to his face. She hated the taste of raw onions, and most times, Suya vendors added extra onions instead of beef to deceive their customers.

"Open your mouth," she said when he just stared at her blankly. "What, street food is too lowly for your divine highness?" she teased.

When Ṣango opened his mouth to respond to her jab, she shoved the meat in and laughed as he widened his eyes in surprise.

Defeated, he shut his mouth and chewed slowly, shooting daggers at her with his gaze. Yet, soon enough, the spicy taste of the barbecue seeped into his senses, and he understood why she had looked like she was on Cloud Nine.

"Whoah! This… this…"

Toyin could only laugh at his stupefaction, and he ignored her and turned to the vendor.

"I want it all," he ordered.

Chapter Seventeen

Toyin hadn't stopped laughing since they left Suya Junction. She'd had to stop Ṣango from buying out the entire place, and he was still sulking.

"Are you seriously not going to speak to me?" she asked, trying to stop herself from laughing, which was, of course, futile, and her eyes watered from the effort. "What were you going to do with that amount of meat?"

"What else am I going to do with it?"

At this point, she couldn't hold it anymore and burst out laughing. "You need to see the look on your face."

Ṣango looked affronted. He paused and stared at her. "You love to laugh, do you not?"

She stopped. "Why are you looking at me like that?" She took a step back as he menacingly approached her. "Stop it."

"Stop what?" he asked, a mischievous grin playing at the corners of his lips.

"I don't know, whatever it is you are thinking of doing." She took another cautious step back.

Ṣango caught up to her in two strides and tickled her.

"Oh pl... pl... Please," she barely choked out amid the laughter.

"You are ticklish, just as I thought." He smirked.

"We are on the street, and people are watching."

But he was relentless.

"This is what you get for laughing at a deity," he said, smirking down at her when he finally stopped tickling her.

"I'm going to get you back for this."

Toyin could feel the eyes of passersby on her, and she didn't mind, strangely enough. She held on to Ṣango's hand to keep from falling, her legs still quivering from her spurt of laughter.

Ṣango put his arm around her shoulders and drew her in as they walked back towards the apartment building. She willingly leaned into him, enjoying the warmth from his body. Deciding to walk back to the apartment had been his idea. She suspected it was because he enjoyed being under the open sky more than anything else.

"You should laugh more often," he said. "The sound of your laughter is beautiful."

"I laugh all the time." She smiled.

"No, not really, you do not. There is an underlying sadness about you since I have met you. It seems like you are going through life forcing happiness, but it does not go in deep. Is it about that lover of yours?"

She scoffed at the mention of Ṣẹyẹ. She hadn't thought about him in days, which was weird because he had been the centre of her world since they were kids, dating through university, being with him through her depressive episodes. But deep down, her sadness originated from way back. From the day her father — her first and best friend — had died.

Ṣango sighed and drew her in. It didn't occur to her that they were violating the number one rule on the list they had made.

"I think that's where it began, or maybe it was after my mother's illness began, I don't know, but sometimes, it just feels like the universe is punishing me for something I did or didn't do, and then is using the ones I love to get back at me."

"The universe does not punish people," he said quietly.

"Ah, you would know that, wouldn't you?"

He laughed. "We are home."

"Oh," Toyin said with the sad realisation their evening together had come to an end.

They ascended the stairs of the building quietly. She also noticed he was no longer touching her, his hands now shoved into the pockets of his trousers. She missed the warmth of his arm around her shoulders, and she shamelessly admitted to herself she wanted to kiss him.

Still, she was the one who'd insisted on the rules because she wasn't sure how dallying with a supernatural being was going to end. She watched him through her peripheral vision, hoping to the high heavens he wasn't reading her mind because that would be utterly embarrassing.

"I am not reading your mind, I promise," he said with a smirk across his lips.

Toyin felt scandalised. "Then why did you say that at the exact moment I thought it?"

Ṣango laughed, that deep-throated laugh she had come to love in the short space of time.

"It's not funny."

"Oh, it is. Trust me."

Toyin crossed her arms and raised an eyebrow at him. They were now in the lobby, standing in front of the passage their apartments shared.

"When I make a promise, I keep it, Órèkelèwá. But I could tell you were thinking about it by the way you kept glancing at me all through our ascent up those ridiculous stairs."

She laughed. It was true she kept glancing at him, and now that her question had been answered, an awkward silence descended on them.

"I guess it's goodnight, then." She stared at her toes, suddenly unable to meet his eyes.

"I guess it is."

Ṣango stepped close to her, close enough to cup her chin and lift it so she now looked into his eyes. They were dark and unreadable. The dim bulb in the lobby added to the effect of the darkness around him.

"Ṣango," she breathed. "The rules...." But she couldn't bring herself to protest entirely.

"You would have to forgive me just this once." He leaned towards her and placed a kiss on her forehead. "This is as far as I will go this time, at least, until you are ready," he said as he stepped away from her.

Toyin smiled weakly, bade him good night one more time, and then went into her apartment, her heart thumping wildly within her ribcage.

***

Ṣango's smile disappeared as soon as Toyin shut the door behind her, the affectionate look on his face replaced with a sinister expression.

"How long are you going to keep hiding?" His amber eyes glowed fiercely as he turned to face the form materialising out of dark clouds and mist in the lobby.

"My Lord." The figure gave a curt, mock bow and stood back up with the slyest look in his eyes and a mischievous grin spreading across his face. He had the face and body of Ṣeye, Toyin's ex-boyfriend, but Ṣango knew better.

"What are you doing here, Timi?" he asked, grinding his teeth to keep a leash on his temper because the last thing he wanted was to burn down the entire building along with Toyin in it. She wasn't a goddess and would never survive the wrath of his fire.

"That was beautiful to see," Timi said, ignoring his question as he walked up to him. "Is that her, the woman who is to help you find your Ọṣẹ?"

"How did you know to find me here?" Ṣango asked, directing the conversation away from Toyin.

"Oh, please, did you really believe anything could stay hidden in Ìlú Òrìṣà, where spirits roam about as they please, listening to conversations and selling them for favours? Spirits even a powerful god as yourself has no control over."

"You paid a wavering spirit to spy on me?" Ṣango found himself rolling his eyes in the way Toyin would have. "Your treachery has no bounds. I can see why you have chosen this human as your host. You are both despicable."

Something dropped in Toyin's apartment, and Ṣango cocked his head towards the sound, briefly breaking his promise not to intrude on her privacy. After making sure she was all right, he turned back to face Timi.

"Let us continue this outside." He grabbed the collar of his shirt, and they both disappeared and materialised on the roof of the building.

"Ah, I see you still have it in you." Timi smirked.

"My Ọṣẹ́ is not the source of my powers, I am the source of my Ọṣẹ́'s power. And I have the mind to smite you to pieces right now." Ṣango let go of Timi's collar with the expression of a man who'd realised he had stepped into a pile of faeces.

He stared at Timi, seething, with his eyes growing redder by the second. Lightning flashed, and thunder rumbled.

"Careful now, my Lord. We do not want to destroy the human world, do we?"

"You have done enough. The little stunt you pulled with Ẹṣu could very well end the world, and you dare to show up in front of me."

"The world can go to pieces, for all I care. Humans are ungrateful little chits, anyway. Just look at how they treat Earth that houses and feeds them; they do not deserve to be here."

Ṣango scoffed. Since when did Timi care about the Earth? Of all the ungrateful beings in the world, Timi topped the list.

"But what I do want is to defeat you in battle, to see your back on the ground and watch you dissipate as my weapon plunges into your heart." Timi was almost frothing at the mouth as the intensity of the hate he felt towards Ṣango formed a dark cloud around him.

Ṣango, despite his anger, felt himself laugh. His eyes cooled down as he laughed harder, to Timi's dismay and confusion.

"What is funny?"

"You. You are what is funny."

Timi's eyes widened. "I have been your friend, your brother, your soldier, your enemy. I have been many things to you, but I have never been your jester."

"You should have been. It is a role that suits you better than any you have ever played in my life," Ṣango said pointedly. He was no longer angry, just amused as to how pointless his feud with Timi had been all these years.

Timi had betrayed him and had almost taken his life. But now, standing there on the roof, in light of everything that had happened and was still happening, he realised he didn't care about Timi anymore. He wanted to stop the world from ending not because he cared about humans but because of Toyin. He wanted to ease her sadness, bring a little joy into her life.

"Oh, I am going to enjoy destroying you, and you will not be laughing by the time I am through with you."

Ṣango scoffed and turned his back. "You need to stop because whether or not I find my Oṣé, there is nothing you can do to me."

"You never learn, do you?"

Ṣango kept walking. For the first time in centuries, he was determined to ignore Timi. He had humoured him for too long, and that's what had led to this mess.

"I wonder just how strong your new human pet is."

Ṣango paused in his tracks and slowly turned to face Timi.

"Now I have your attention." Timi snickered. "You see, the problem with it is that you never take me seriously. You are in love with her, are you not? Why do you always do these things when you know it will never end well?" Timi was smirking as he circled Ṣango. "You always make things easy for me."

Ṣango gritted his teeth and balled his fists.

"You will not lay a finger on Toyin. You will leave her be, or I swear to everything hidden in the skies and everything hidden underneath the earth that I will end your spiteful existence, and it would not be for the amusement of Ìlú Òrìṣà."

Timi stopped pacing and looked into Ṣango's burning amber eyes.

"You seem afraid rather than angry, my lord. Are you scared that I might take her away and turn her against you like I did with Ọya?"

"Timi..." Ṣango groaned, a warning that flew over Timi's head.

"I am going to enjoy this. She will never love you, you are never going to get your Oṣé back, the world can go to smithereens for all I care, but I will be the end of you."

Ṣango yelled. Sparks of fire flew out of his mouth. His eyes turned red as he lurched for his enemy's neck, but Timi dissolved with a smirk into dark mist.

Ṣango yelled his frustration into the night. The weight of his anger caused lightning to strike an electricity pole, sending the entire street and beyond into a blackout.

CHAPTER EIGHTEEN

Toyin sat on the edge of her bed, phone in hand, and dialled her mother's number. Talking about her father's death with Ṣango had made her miss her mother. Guilt gripped her heart as the phone rang. She barely checked in on her or even visited her, only sent her money for her upkeep. Her father's death had broken them both irreparably. And for a long while after, life became uneventful, the spark having disappeared. The stories stopped, the laughter died—they had lived but had barely been alive. Then her mother had gotten sick—she'd had a stroke, and it had been too painful for Toyin to visit her or even speak to her.

Her mother picked up just on the third ring. "Ṣangotoyin mi."

My Ṣangotoyin. She loved it when her mother called her that. It gave her a sense of belonging, reassured no matter how strained their relationship, her mother loved her.

"M...mama." She could barely form the words, her tongue heavy as she fought back the tears.

"Is everything okay, my baby?"

Her mother's speech was slightly slurred due to the stroke she'd had years ago, but the affection and concern she felt for her daughter still rang evident in her voice.

Toyin cleared her throat and tried again. "I miss you, Mama."

"I miss you, too, my baby, but I'm fine, and I'm taking my drugs. The nurse you sent to take care of me is very nice, too. Is everything okay in Lagos?"

"Everything is fine, Mama. I'll come and see you as—"

"No, no, don't come here, Ṣangotoyin mi. The aura of this place doesn't suit you."

Toyin laughed at that response. It was the first time in years since she'd heard her mother talk about auras.

"Mama, are you back to being the spirit woman?" she joked and then bit her lip at the error she had just made. Her father, when he was alive, used to call her mother *Spirit Woman*, because she believed she was a descendant of an ancient powerful cult of Ṣango worshippers, the *Baba Mogba*. Back then when life was simpler and her mother used to believe in stories, the endearment used to make her smile no matter how upset she was. An awkward silence followed before she apologised. "I'm sorry, Mama. I didn't mean to say that.

"Oh, no, no, my darling. There is nothing to be sorry about. We have let the heavy cloud caused by your father's death hang over us for too long. It's time we moved on. And to answer your question, yes, I am back to being the spirit woman."

"What?" Toyin laughed.

"An ancestor visited me in my dream recently. I told you I am a descendant of women and men who wielded powerful magic in the ancient days."

She smiled. Funny how fast the night changes. She used to laugh at her parents for being superstitious and a bit weird, but now, with a supernatural being living just opposite her, it would be stupid of her not to believe her mother.

"I hope she is a comfort to you," she said, and her mother laughed. It was the first time in years hearing her mother laugh, and it gladdened her heart.

"Ah, she mostly tells me stories. Her words are twisted in riddles and prophecies. When I'm awake, I try to decipher the meaning behind her words. I write them down in my journal."

"Isn't that too much stress for you?"

"Bah. It gives me something to do."

"But—"

"Ṣangotoyin mi, don't worry about me. I'm finally living after all these years, and I want you to do the same, too. You have to let go of the sadness that has enslaved you since your father left us. It was his fate to leave the way he did, and it was no fault of ours. I want you to be happy. I want you to find a man that would love you as much and even more than your father loved me."

Toyin scoffed. The African woman in her mother just had to jump out—she found a way to bring up marriage.

"Mama, if you are alluding to Ṣẹyẹ and me getting married, that's not going to happen because we broke up."

"Thanks to the skies. I could not stand that boy. Finally!"

"Mama!" Toyin couldn't hide the surprise in her tone. "You never once said anything about it."

"You looked happy with him, and considering how I shut down after your father died, I didn't think I had the right to interfere in your love life or any part of your life, for that matter. But, my baby, you are a great woman. You have some important part to play in the world. Your grandmother saw it, and I sensed it, too, and you need a great man by your side, a great man who would love you like you deserve to be loved."

"Mama…" The tears were threatening to spill again. Her mother had seen through Ṣẹyẹ but had kept quiet because she felt the same guilt Toyin was also feeling.

"I love you, Mama," was all she could manage to say. She couldn't trust herself to say anything more without bursting into tears.

"I love you, too, my baby. I need to go now. Your nurse is giving me the stare down because I should be in bed."

"Oh, I didn't mean to keep you this long. Goodnight, Mama."

Several minutes after the call had ended, Toyin remained sitting in the same position musing over the conversation with her mother. Her mother wanted her to have a great man by her side. She scoffed. More like a great god.

She caught herself and then stopped smiling. Somehow, the thought of spending the rest of her life with Ṣango by her side had crept up on her. Ridiculous how the idea seemed normal to her because she knew nothing would come out of it—he was here for a purpose, and sooner or later, he would leave because gods weren't supposed to roam the earth among humans.

But even that thought didn't ease the sweet feeling inside her when she thought about how it would feel to spend the rest of her life with Ṣango by her side. Her existence would be filled with banter and laughter and sweet kisses.

"That's not a bad life to have, is it?" she asked the stuffed panda occupying a considerable amount of space on her bed and smiled, then patted it on the head when she didn't get any response.

Her parched throat reminded her she'd eaten a lot of barbecued beef without drinking any water. On her way to the kitchen, giddy with excitement for some reason, she tripped on her own feet and caught herself before hitting the ground. But she couldn't save her phone from the same fate. She panicked for a bit as she picked it up and heaved a sigh of relief when she examined it and confirmed it was fine. She was still paying for it and could not afford to get a new phone if this one was damaged. Her mother's bills were taking a considerable amount of her monthly income.

After her thirst was satisfied, she brushed her teeth and took a quick shower to remove the lingering odour of Suya from her body and then settled in for the night. She wondered what Ṣango was doing now. Gbonka had probably already returned, and they were discussing strategies for finding Ṣango's Oṣé or some other divine stately affairs, whatever that meant.

A thought occurred to her, and she smiled sheepishly to herself as she typed in the search word on Google. Her Google search was still loading when she heard a loud spark followed by a total blackout.

"This transformer has blown again. Only God knows what century light will come back on in this neighbourhood," she said, kissing her teeth as she leaned over to her side and turned on the LED rechargeable bed lamp on her side drawer. She then returned to her already loaded Google page, and a broad smile filled her face.

"Ṣango is going to be so surprised when I do this." She flushed.

***

Gbonka stood before Ṣango looking tattered and dishevelled and somewhat ashamed of himself.

"I am sorry, my Lord, I got caught in his web of deceit. It took me a while to free myself from it."

Ṣango waved his apology away. He wasn't going to blame him for something that wasn't his fault. Timi was a master of deceit. It was what killed him, and now that he was a demi-god, it had become one of his strengths and powers. He could literally spin a web of deceit — best to avoid getting caught up in it because you had to be mentally strong to be free of it, which was why he didn't want him anywhere near Toyin.

"We have bigger problems than that, Gbonka. Sit down." Ṣango was sitting with his legs crossed on one of the immaculate couches, his brows furrowed in thought.

"My Lord?"

"How many days do we have 'til the deadline?"

"About two weeks."

"I need to end this business before then. I realised that I have been a little selfish in my thoughts," he stated.

Gbonka, despite himself, raised an eyebrow.

"I will smite you to pieces if you make one snide comment about what I just said," Ṣango warned, but it didn't carry the weight of his anger, and Gbonka stifled a laugh.

"I have lived for far too long, and I have somewhat come to terms with the world ending. But for humans, it is not quite the same. Their lives are short, and they live for the little things that give them joy. The world ending because of a cruel joke and a long-time enmity between the gods when they had no part in it would be unfair to them. I mean, they have goals and dreams and—"

"Pardon my interruption, my Lord. By they, you mean Toyin, do you not?"

Ṣango was silent.

"Is this what I think it is?"

This time, Ṣango threw the full weight of his glare at him. "I do not know whatever it is you are thinking. Now focus."

"Yes, my Lord." This time, Gbonka didn't try to hide his smile.

"All Timi wants is to defeat me in battle. He does not care if the world ends, and I have to prevent that and make sure I shut him forever, because I cannot have this happening again."

"I do not think Olódùmarè would watch and let all creatures suffer over this cruel game Timi's playing. At some point, They would have to intervene, do you not think?"

Ṣango stared at his friend blankly for a few seconds, amazed at his naivety. He'd been a demi-god for centuries now, and he still had such romantic beliefs.

"You know how They can be. It's within Their power to return my Oṣé and end of all this nonsense, but that would be making things easy. Even though it was Eṣu's cunning that got out of hand and Timi's viciousness that caused this, I was also careless in underestimating the depth of Timi's hate for me. In other words, it is all our fault. Olódùmarè might interfere before all the world forgets about our existence, but if that happens, even Oṣun's intercessory powers will not be able to save us as it would mean They have interfered with the balance between love and hate because at the end of the day, this is what it is all about. And if there was anything They hated the most, it was interfering with the balance of the world."

Ṣango's face was grim. Things were getting more and more complicated. It had been irritating but simple when Oṣun had explained what he needed to do to have his Oṣé returned. He'd thought all he had to do was find the woman, charm her into loving him, and then he would return to throw the full weight of his anger on Timi and Eṣu. Not like there was anything he could do to Eṣu, who was also a very powerful deity.

He hadn't expected to meet with a strongheaded woman, and worse, even fall in love with her.

He paused and looked, bewildered, at Gbonka. Timi had hinted at it. Hell, even Gbonka had, but he hadn't taken them any seriously. Yet, the realisation of his feelings shocked him more than anything ever had. He enjoyed being with her, was sexually attracted to her, but hadn't thought it was something as serious as love.

"My Lord, is everything all right?" Gbonka asked, concern clouding his face.

"No, no, I am not all right. This is bad, really bad."

"Of course it is bad. That is why we are—"

"No, not that. It is happening all over again."

Sango gripped his heart as the pain engulfed his chest, making it hard for him to breathe. The veins on his neck bulged at the effort it took for him to breathe.

Gbonka was by his side in an instant. "My Lord, my Lord…"

Sango's eyes rolled backward, and he lost consciousness for the second time in the history of his existence.

"This is really bad." Gbonka had to agree.

CHAPTER NINETEEN

Toyin woke up smiling for the first time in years. Not even in the time spent with Ṣẹyẹ had she woken feeling as good as she did this morning. A combination of things were responsible for the beautiful feeling inside her. Her date with Ṣango, her phone conversation with her mother, and her Google search last night.

She couldn't wait to see Ṣango's face when she—

Her thoughts were interrupted by the sound of her doorbell ringing. Smiling, she got out of bed and stretched. Ṣango had been so polite and had been careful not to cross boundaries with her ever since she'd drawn up those rules. She chuckled. Those rules were quite ridiculous—even she had to admit that.

She opened the door, smiling, only for that smile to disappear with abrupt disappointment when she saw who stood there.

"I didn't think that a day would come when you wouldn't be happy to see me," Ṣẹyẹ said and pushed himself into her apartment.

Toyin was both exasperated and surprised. Ṣẹyẹ was not the best man, but he had never been rude.

"I don't remember inviting you in." She turned to face him with her hands crossed over her chest and the door left open so that he knew she wanted him to leave.

He ignored her, and with a smirk, plopped himself on her couch and looked around as if it was his first time here.

She sighed and shut the door, seeing there was no hope of getting him out of her place without scruffles, and she wasn't about to let any of her nosy neighbours see inside. Although, it was not so surprising that they had left her alone ever since Ṣango had moved in.

"What do you want, really?"

"Can't I visit my girlfriend?"

His eyes cut to her, and she could almost swear she saw something shift in his irises. However, she shook it away. Ever since Ṣango had come to her life, she had become overly sensitive; she now read meanings into plain and ordinary things.

"Ex-girlfriend, and no, you can't just barge into my house anytime you like."

"I didn't barge. I used the doorbell, and you opened. I could have used my keys."

"I changed the locks."

At that, Ṣẹyẹ sighed and got to his feet, hands in the pockets of his jeans, and walked towards her. Toyin instinctively took a step back. She wasn't sure what it was, but something was different. Something sinister hovered about him.

"We can't just throw all those years we've had together away like that," he began.

"Look—"

"I'm sorry, Toyin."

The intensity of his apology took her aback and left her lost for words.

"I was insensitive, and stupid, and honestly, I don't know what came over me to ask you to choose between having your career goals and me, knowing fully well how much it means to you."

Toyin was silent. She hadn't expected to see him so soon after their encounter at the supermarket. Also, she hadn't anticipated the apology.

"Ṣẹyẹ, I don't know what you want me to say..." she trailed off, letting her hands fall to her sides as she slightly shook her head. "I'll accept your apology, but things are different now, and we can't go back to being who we were before. That ship has sailed."

"Why?" he asked, his voice solemn.

She could even see the tears threatening to spill from his eyes. It caused a stir in her heart to see him that way.

"I think you need to leave. It's too early in the morning for me to deal with this."

She made to open the door, but he pulled her back, his hands wrapped around her waist as he held her tightly.

"Please, baby. It's us. We have been through hell together, and we can't just let it go like that."

The freshness of his breath engulfed her, yet it was the intense look in his eyes that left her paralysed and unable to protest as his lips met hers. It was light at first, a gentle caress, then his tongue pushed into her mouth. To her own surprise, she found herself opening herself to him.

This kiss was different from any they'd ever had before, with some sort of life and passion burning as their tongues danced sensually. There was a need, a powerful force that seemed to draw her into an endless spool of desire.

That's how she knew. Her eyes flew open, and she shoved him away.

"I don't know who you are, but you need to get out now!" she yelled at him and took several steps away.

His eyes flickered, and the darkness she had suspected earlier covered his eyes completely.

"You are quite stronger than I imagined." A sly grin played at the corner of his mouth. His voice seemed to be coming from far away when he was standing right in front her.

"Who are you, and what have you done to Ṣẹyẹ?" Underneath her brave words, she was shaking inside.

"Hmm." He scoffed and wiped his lips with his thumb, which he then rubbed nonchalantly with his index finger. "You taste so good, just like her. I can see why Ṣango is in over his head for you," he said, looking back up at her, still grinning.

At the mention of Ṣango's name, Toyin had a faint idea who the being before her might be. She wished for the first time that Ṣango was lurking in her mind, that he could feel her fear and come to her rescue. Screaming might help her achieve this, yet for some reason, she couldn't find her voice. She just stood there, shivering, her back against the door.

"Oh, come on. I am not going to hurt you. You are much too valuable to me. I just wanted to see what it is about you that held the master of fire's interest, and now I know."

His dark eyes unnerved her beyond words could explain.

"Wh—" Toyin began then couldn't quite form the words so she took a deep breath and tried again. "What did you do to Ṣeyẹ? Where is he?"

She wasn't sure he'd heard her question because her voice was so low, it couldn't even be called a whisper, and the blank expression on his face also confirmed this.

And then, he smiled—a smile even more unnerving than his sinister grin.

"Oh, you mean the human who was nice enough to loan me his body." He stepped a bit closer, and Toyin resisted the urge to shut her eyes. "He is in there somewhere. He will wander for a while, imprisoned in his own mind, until I am done with his body, although I am not sure he will survive it. He would be nothing more than a vegetable. A crazy vegetable," he said and laughed at his own joke.

"You are a monster," Toyin spat at him.

"Oh, darling, I know, but this monster will become a god soon."

He lightly stroked her chin, and Toyin froze as the contact prickled her skin.

"I shall be back," he said, standing so close, she felt the hotness of his breath, and disappeared into a mist of darkness, leaving her unable to breathe for the next few seconds.

***

Toyin took in a huge breath and raced the short distance between her door to Ṣango's apartment, banging on the panel frantically.

It swung open, and she brushed aside a dishevelled Gbonka and rushed into the room.

"He was here…" she managed, then took a moment to gasp for air.

"Who was?" Gbonka scratched his bald head, looking confused and extremely tired.

"Oh, I don't know what he is, but he was dark. Very, very, very dark," she blurted out as she filled her lungs with enough breath to help her brain function.

Gbonka looked confused for a second. Then understanding chased the confusion, followed by rage. Rage she didn't think sweet and thoughtful albeit buff and strong Gbonka was capable of emitting.

"Where is he?"

"He disappeared. He just…" She shuddered, and her skin prickled at the encounter. "Where's Ṣango? That was the guy responsible for the disappearance of his Oṣé, right?"

"Yes, yes." Gbonka nodded and leaned against the immaculate wall of the apartment.

Only then did she notice the exhaustion radiating from him, slowly burning out the rage he'd previously shown her.

"How did everything come to be such a huge mess?" he asked, but the question wasn't directed at her.

Toyin sighed, too. Just last night, she had been reeling in the happiness of her date with the lord of thunder and fire, and now… Her skin prickled again. She could still feel the coldness of his lingering touch on her neck and the bitterness that kissing him had left her with.

"Where's Ṣango?" she asked again, realising Gbonka hadn't answered her initial question.

He turned slowly to look at her and smiled sadly. "You should leave, Toyin. You are the last person Ṣango should be seeing at this moment."

Those words stung more painfully than angry hornets would if their nest were disturbed.

Ṣango didn't want to see her.

She wanted to ask why, but just as she opened her mouth, Gbonka spoke again.

"I shall put up protective wards in and outside your apartment. It is not much, but it would prevent him from getting in easily."

The way he watched her proved irksome — he looked at her with pity, and she turned away from him and towards the door.

She paused and turned back to face him, anger boiling in the pit of her stomach.

"You know I did not ask to be thrown in the middle of this fight between the gods. I was just sitting on my own, when you people decided to play some silly games with my life by putting the fate of the world in my hands —"

"I am not particularly sure that is how —"

"Let me finish!"

Gbonka snapped his mouth shut at the command.

"You people cannot just be pushing me around anyhow. Whatever that thing was, it could have killed me. He's holding Ṣẹyẹ trapped in his own body. It is the most afraid and creeped out I have felt in a long time, so you people cannot, will not, dismiss me like this."

Gbonka closed his eyes and sighed. "I did not mean to offend you, Toyin. It is just that Ṣango —"

"If Ṣango doesn't want to see me, let him tell me that himself. Until then, I am not leaving until I get some answers."

"That is the thing. It is not that he does not want to see you. He cannot see you."

"What do you mean, he cannot see me?"

"Come and see for yourself," Gbonka said and walked towards Ṣango's room.

Toyin followed him, each step she took heavier than the last.

CHAPTER TWENTY

Ṣango lay on his bed as still as death. Toyin swallowed nervously and looked from his unconscious body to Gbonka who stood behind her with a grim expression.

"I thought you said he doesn't sleep," she stated.

Even she knew she sounded a bit stupid, because the fiery lord looked anything but asleep, even though he was tucked under the covers of his bed. She turned back to look at him, and a shiver ran up her spine. Only then did she realise how deathly cold it was inside Ṣango's room.

"Why is he lying there like that?" she whispered as she leaned over him and placed a hand on his forehead and immediately snatched it back. His body was painfully cold to touch.

Her eyes widened, and panic coated her voice as she repeated her question to Gbonka. "Why the hell is he like this?"

"It is not my place to tell you why he ended up like this." Gbonka's words were low — so low, Toyin barely heard him. "This is the second time in the centuries he has lived that he has turned out like this. However, the first time, he was out for only a couple of minutes, but he has been like this since last night."

"But… I don't understand. How?"

"You cannot stay here. The temperature keeps dropping, and I do not think—"

"I'm not going anywhere," she snapped at Gbonka, not for the first time today. She saw the wounded look in his eyes and quickly apologised. "I'm sorry. There is just so much happening at the same time. I know it's not an excuse for my behaviour. I'm sorry."

"I understand. You and Ṣango are tethered by Ọṣun, so it is normal for you to feel extra peevish. The fire in Ṣango is dying out slowly."

"Dying out?"

Gbonka only smiled sadly. "I will give you a few minutes with him, but that is all I can do. If his fire gets reignited and he wakes up to find you passed out from hypothermia, he would have my hide."

He nodded curtly and then left her alone with the frozen lord of thunder.

"This is all my fault," she whispered, tears sliding down her cheeks. Her lips trembled from the cold. "Your fire is dying because of me, because I can't help you get your Ọṣé back. The world is beginning to forget you completely, aren't they?"

Guilt and a certain type of pain she had never felt before gripped her heart. She held her chest and let the tears flow.

It was fear—fear that Ṣango was slipping out of this world, fear that she would never see him again. That she would never see his arrogant smirk, or hear his rich laughter, or hear him call her Órèkelèwá. She would never feel the warmth from his body again, warmth she had pushed away over and over.

Without thinking, she got under the covers with him. If only his fire were to reignite, if only temporarily, just so she could tell him how happy his presence, however short in her life, had made her and how sorry she was for being too selfish to love him, too selfish to save him and save the world. Then, she would use whatever warmth her body could provide to aid him.

And if his fire would never come back and the world went to pieces, then there was no place she'd rather be when the world ended than here, with her arms around him.

She lifted his head gently off the pillow and placed it on her chest and wrapped her arms around his shoulders and his leg in between her legs.

"I'm so sorry," she apologised as she lightly traced his pale face, the cold biting her fingers. He had always been unnaturally warm to touch, but today, he was just the opposite.

She yawned, and her eyes slowly got too heavy for her to keep them open. She didn't know how much time had passed, probably not a lot if Gbonka hadn't come for her, yet for her to be already feeling sleepy, it must mean the temperature in the room had dropped even lower. She let sleep take her, knowing full well she may never wake up again. Her last thoughts were of her mother and how she never got to say goodbye.

Regrets. She had too many regrets…

***

Even without opening her eyes, Toyin slowly became aware of her surroundings. She noticed she was warm and nicely tucked under the covers, with her head resting comfortably on the plush pillows.

Her first thought was that the world had ended and she had died and was now in Heaven, then she remembered how, if the world ended in that way, there would be no Heaven. She snuggled deeper under the covers and heard a chuckle.

A very familiar chuckle, and a familiar situation. Her eyes flew open to find a very alive and very warm Ṣango watching her with his head propped up on his hand, the infamous glint in his amber eyes, and a mischievous grin playing at the corner of his lips. He still wore the clothes he'd had on last night, or the last night they'd met, because she couldn't tell how long she had been asleep.

Her heart lifted in joy to see him alive and well, and relief that his fire had been reignited coursed through—now, both him and the world had a fighting chance. Then her brain registered they were both in bed together, their legs still entwined under the covers.

Her eyes widened, and she attempted to fly out of the bed. Ṣango gently but firmly pushed her back on the mattress with his free hand.

"Not so fast, Órèkelèwá. Not so fast."

Her insides melted as those words rolled off his tongue, and she smiled up sweetly at him.

"For someone with a strictly no-touching rule, you were all over me this morning. What am I supposed to make of that?" he asked teasingly, his eyes holding hers captive and bewitched.

"What do you want to make of it?" she teased back, and her seductive tone surprised her.

He merely smiled and stroked the side of her face lightly. "I want to kiss you so badly."

"What's stopping you?"

"Because if I do, I would not want to stop." His amber eyes grew dark as he caressed her face with his light strokes.

"I wouldn't want you stop."

The finger stroking her face stopped, and his eyes searched her face. "Toyin, I am—"

She silenced the rest of his words by leaning slightly off the bed and placing a tentative nibble on his lips. She leaned back and watched a small smile play at the corner of his lips.

"Are you sure you will not regret this?" he asked, still restraining himself.

"I'm done with regrets," she said softly and leaned up to kiss him again, this time deeply.

He responded with equal enthusiasm, and she felt every restraint he had over himself let go as he deepened his exploration of her mouth and moved fully on top of her. Toyin wrapped her legs around his, pulling him closer onto her body.

He peeled his lips off her mouth and trailed light caresses down her neck while his hands slid under her nightdress that had already ridden far above her thighs. When they found her breasts, she moaned at the contact, her nipples rising to the attention Ṣango was giving them.

He returned his attention to her lips and then paused, studying her face with a half-smile on his lips.

"Why did you stop? I don't want you to stop," she said, her voice husky and heavy with passion. She leaned up to continue, but he stopped her with his hand and chuckled.

"Patience, Órèkelèwá."

He gently stripped off her nightdress and tossed it away, then pressed a quick, deep kiss on her mouth before he proceeded to rid himself of his own clothes. Toyin's eyes widened, and she sucked in a breath at the gorgeousness of his body. She reached out to touch his lean muscles, but he clucked his tongue and held her hand and gently pressed her back onto the bed.

"I want to taste you. Every part of you," he said.

Toyin shuddered in pleasurable anticipation.

He kissed her again on the mouth, nibbling on her lips gently, then trailed his teeth and tongue down her neck. Each graze sent little tremors between her legs, and when his mouth lowered to her breast, and he took a nipple into his mouth, flicking it as he sucked, she ran her fingers into his hair and arched her back at the insane pleasure his tongue gave her before he moved to give her other breast the same attention.

And just when she thought it couldn't get any better than this, he directed his kisses down her stomach, stopping to briefly to nibble on her navel. She dug her fingers into his head, and Ṣango let out an amused groan yet didn't stop his assault of caresses until he got to her centre.

The first feel of his tongue on her clit nearly sent her over the edge, and Toyin found herself shivering.

"You taste just as delicious as I imagined you would," he said against her pussy before he proceeded to completely devour her, savouring the taste of her juices. He stroked her clit as he slid his tongue in and out of her, making her twist and turn and shiver.

Just when she was at the edge, he stopped.

She let out a moan of disappointment and watched him through clouded eyes as he brought himself over her.

"I want you to taste yourself as you let go."

And without giving her time to process what he had meant by those words, he slammed his mouth against hers and slid his fingers into her pussy. She moaned hungrily against his mouth, tasting herself on him and fully grasping the meaning of the word 'delicious."

His fingers pumped in and out of her, sending waves of pleasure into every part of her body until it could not keep on anymore, and her climax came crashing down on her powerfully like ocean waves on a stormy day. Only then did he stop kissing her, so she could catch her breath. He slowly slid his fingers out of her as she spasmed against him.

"You are so beautiful," he whispered and licked the tear sliding down her temple into her ear.

Toyin hadn't even realised she'd been crying. If having his tongue and his fingers inside her made her feel this way, she wondered just how crazy the full length of him inside her would drive her.

She didn't have to wonder for long. As her spasms eased off, he gently replaced his fingers with his cock. He slid in gently and carefully, allowing her pussy time to adjust to the considerable length of him. She could see in the strain on his face what the cautiousness was costing him, so she encouraged him by lifting her hips higher and closer to him, allowing him unrestrained access into her body.

He took her mouth with his and let out a pleasurable groan as he buried himself to the hilt inside and began to thrust. Slowly at first, savouring and enjoying every moment of their joining, and then faster and faster, their breaths trying desperately to match up to the pace of their lovemaking, until Toyin climaxed again, gripping onto Ṣango tightly as her release overcame her.

And not to long after, his orgasm came, just as powerful as her own, and he moaned to that effect into her ear and said something afterwards.

Something Toyin wasn't sure she heard correctly because her brain was still so scrambled, but she decided to not ask, at least not now. Now, she allowed Ṣango to wrap his arms around her as she rested her head on his chest and lazily stroked his pecs, waiting for the regret and shame of what she had just done to hit her.

But they never did. What hit her instead was the realisation that she hadn't eaten anything that day as her stomach grumbled, and Ṣango laughed. In that moment, all felt right and perfect with the world.

CHAPTER TWENTY-ONE

"Let us get you something to eat, before your stomach brings down the whole house." Ṣango laughed as he got out of bed.

"Oh, please. If I didn't bring down the house while you were inside me, the grumbling of my stomach can hardly compare."

Ṣango only smirked as he picked up his trousers from the floor and put them on.

"Hmm…" Toyin purred, and he turned to look at her only to find her staring at him like he was a meal she wanted to devour, a pout on her face, her chin placed on her upturned palms as she watched him.

"What?"

"Do you really have to put on your clothes?"

He furrowed his brows slightly in confusion.

"I mean, why would you want to cover up this beautiful body? I could stare at you all day and not get tired."

"What?" He laughed. In all his years, he had never, ever flushed in front of anyone. He cleared his throat to hide the fact as he pulled on his trousers.

"You little tease."

"Tease? I haven't even done anything yet. You didn't let me explore your body the way I wanted to. Next time, I'll do what I want, and then you will learn the definition of tease."

"Ah ah!" Ṣango put his hands on his hips and stared at her in amazement. He'd known a tempered fire burned underneath, yet seeing this side of her proved surprising, even more surprising than her moaning his name just a few minutes ago.

"Keep talking like that, and we are never going to leave this room," he said as he picked up his shirt.

"At least, don't wear a shirt nau."

She blinked up at him from the bed, still pouting. He wanted so badly to kiss those full, beautiful lips of hers, but he knew where that would lead to, and she was hungry and they had other matters to take care of.

"This woman…" He sighed as he threw his shirt to her, conceding to leave his trousers on, and then left the room as fast as his legs could carry him though not fast enough to miss her chuckle.

***

In the sitting room, Gbonka was watching a TV show, ear buds in his ears when Ṣango came out of the bedroom.

"*I know you have superhuman strength and hearing, but how exactly does this work?*" he spoke to his mind.

"Ah, finally! You are out," Gbonka said, removing the earbuds and turning on the couch to face Ṣango.

"Care to explain?"

"You really need me to explain to you the noise you and Toyin were making in there? I had to create soundproof wards around the house, to prevent you both from disturbing the whole neighbourhood. Unfortunately, I am immune to my own wards, so…"

"Ah," was all Ṣango said to Gbonka's rants and went into the kitchen.

"Hmm," Gbonka grunted and turned back to the television. "You could just think about what food you want to cook, and it would appear," he yelled towards the kitchen a few minutes later over the clanging and banging of utensils coming from the kitchen. "I am sure the Lord of Thunder knows of his own strength and powers," he added a few seconds later when her didn't get a response from Ṣango.

There was silence for a bit, then Ṣango answered. "Cooking it myself feels more genuine and sincere."

"Of course it would," Gbonka muttered. "Never advise a deity in love."

"I heard that!"

Gbonka simply shook his head and was about to plug his earbuds in again when Toyin came out wearing Ṣango's shirt.

"What's that?" she asked as she plopped onto the couch and folded her legs yoga style.

"That is the sound of the Lord of Fire trying to cook for you. Another way you can look at it is a disaster waiting to happen."

"But he's cooked for me before, and it wasn't disastrous. It tasted fantastic, actually," she countered, and somewhere in the kitchen, Ṣango smiled at her defence of his cooking.

"He might have looked cool cooking for you, but trust me, he had to practice that one meal over and over again. You were asleep for most of the disastrous parts. So much for his super strength and IQ," Gbonka replied.

Ṣango had to fight the urge to go into the living room and clobber him.

Gbonka was right, though. Two hours and several unsuccessful trials later, Toyin had to settle for a bowl of cereal and milk while Gbonka tried very unsuccessfully not to laugh at both of them.

Toyin and Gbonka both filled him in on the incident that had happened this morning with Timi. He listened carefully as she narrated every bit of her encounter with Timi, only raising his eyebrow slightly when she mentioned the kiss. Other than that, he didn't interrupt her.

"That bastard," he said finally when she'd finished.

"You're not mad that I kissed him?"

"Oh, you did not kiss him. He kissed you, and I am going to kill him for it." He had told Timi to stay away from her, but he had gone ahead and done just the opposite.

"He has always been a menace, and he has gotten bolder. He has been totally and absolutely consumed by his hate and greed," Gbonka stated.

"I know, and that is why I am going to end it once and for all."

"How?" both Gbonka and Toyin asked at the same time.

"We will do the old way. I am going to challenge him to a fight."

"Even without your Ọṣẹ, you are going to defeat him, that is not up for contention. But what will that achieve? You always beat him, and every time, he comes back," Gbonka pointed out.

Ṣango didn't say anything for a few seconds, leading both Gbonka and Toyin to believe he wasn't going to answer until he spoke again.

"I have a plan."

He looked directly at Gbonka whose eyes widened at the unspoken errand he had just sent him on. Ṣango shook his head silently as Gbonka moved to argue. He understood his sentiment because he was sending him to the very goddesses he swore he would never have anything to do with again.

Gbonka slowly got to his feet, and with a grim expression, dematerialised.

"Where is he going?" Toyin asked, sounding a little upset to be removed from whatever internal conversation Ṣango and Gbonka had had.

The expression made Ṣango smile.

"He went to deliver a very important message," was all he said even though he knew it would in no way satisfy her curiosity.

"Ah, you are keeping secrets now abi?"

Instead of answering, he simply scooped her from the couch and placed her on his lap like she was no lighter than a toddler.

"Why are you not asking what you really want to ask?" he said and kissed the nape of her neck lightly.

"Because it's my fault," she replied quietly and held his face in her hands as she added, "You are dying, aren't you?"

Ṣango chuckled. "I cannot die, you know that, Órèkelẹ̀wá. And what happened to me last night was not your fault, at least not in the way you think."

Toyin sighed and kissed him on the mouth. He deepened the kiss. They spent the next few minutes sharing the same breath and tasting each other. He had only just started to unbutton his shirt on her when she broke their contact.

"Ah ah!" she said as if just remembering something.

"What is it?" Worry edged into his voice, thinking she had probably remembered an important detail from Timi's unwanted visit.

"I've been meaning to say this for days now," she said, looking at the top of his head.

Ṣango raised an eyebrow.

"We need to do something to your hair, it's rough and—"

"What?" He sat up straighter, unable to believe his ears. "That is what you stopped… what?"

"I'll be right back. Give me a few seconds," she said, leaping off his legs.

"Does it have to be right now?"

"Yes, baby, it does. I'll be right back." She planted a quick but affectionate peck on his forehead and dashed out of the apartment.

If only she hadn't forbidden him from reading her mind, he might have gone into her head just to understand how her mind worked. He was still on that thought when he felt her presence at the door and commanded the panel to open, only for her to come back in with a bunch of colourful containers and a bag full of combs.

She dumped them on the couch beside him. He picked one of the containers, a plastic bottle, and read what was on it.

"Moisturising shampoo…" He then looked back up at her. She was smiling gingerly at him. "You are being serious."

"As serious as death, baby. I have always wondered what your hair would feel like," she said, opening the bag of combs and bringing out a wooden cutting comb.

Ṣango snickered. "You know, when the world was still young, that comb was used to make charms."

"Hmm, that's interesting," Toyin said, hardly paying attention as she leaned over him and began to loosen one of the strands of his cornrows.

Ṣango, who would rather have her pinned beneath him on the couch while he slid in and out of her, begrudgingly let her have her way with his hair. He'd once been a polygamous man, living with three wives—he'd learned long ago what happened when you didn't let women have their way, and Toyin, heavens bless her, had the stubbornness and fire of all the three goddesses he'd once been married to combined.

So he patiently let her unbraid his hair, lead him to the bathroom to wash it, and sat back down as she put in all sorts of oils and creams. Finally, he had to sit through another hour or so of her braiding his hair into a style she called two-strand twists.

He had to admit he quite enjoyed himself during the long and somewhat tedious process. He enjoyed hearing her laugh at some of the ancient stories he told her, some she found difficult to believe. And he did manage to steal kisses at a few points when she bent over him while she worked. In the bathroom, while she washed his hair, he had almost, almost gotten her to abandon her self-imposed mission of tackling his hair. Damn, the woman was tenacious, and while she moaned her pleasure as his fingers slid in and out her, she did not once stop washing his hair.

After Ọya and all that had happened between them, he didn't think he could or that he even wanted to fall in love again, and now that he had, he was glad it was Toyin he had fallen in love with, even though Orí had played a cruel game with him and his time with her was destined to be extremely short.

CHAPTER TWENTY-TWO

After doing Ṣango's hair, they spent the rest of the evening making love. Ṣango sent ripples through her body, gave her orgasm upon orgasm that she unashamedly let take over her. Wrapped against him, in the aftermath of their lovemaking, they breathed in sync.

Toyin knew this feeling; she knew it all too well. It was how she had felt in the beginning with Ṣeye. No, it was better. This feeling, the butterflies, everything was different. This one felt wholesome, fulfilling. It felt true.

She had confirmed her feelings the night before as she scrolled the internet. She understood and accepted what she felt for Ṣango. But she couldn't tell him—she didn't want to raise his hopes because she couldn't give him what he really wanted.

Maybe, in the end, she wasn't really any different from Ṣeye. She was selfish, and as much as Ṣango made her happy and made her feel things she had always thought existed only in romance novels and movies, she couldn't even die for him. No matter how much she loved him, no matter the promise of eternal life.

She didn't want to end up like Gbonka, didn't want to be a demi-god or whatever. She wanted the life she had, wanted to live it to the fullest so that when her time on earth finally came, she would leave with no regrets. That's what she wanted, a life full of love no matter how short it would be. It was why, even though she understood this thing between her and Ṣango was unrealistic and there was no happily ever after waiting for them, she would rather enjoy these moments with him, where she was truly happy and loved, than declare her feelings for him and let him have expectations of her.

Fate can be one cruel bastard to make her find the kind of love she deserved only to demand her death to preserve said love.

"I am going somewhere for a couple of days," Ṣango said, breaking the silence.

Toyin wasn't surprised to hear him say that. She had been expecting him to say something like this.

"Will you come back?" A foolish question, because she knew the end was coming.

"Ọrèkelèwá," he breathed as he turned on his side to face her. He smiled and cupped her cheek. He kissed her forehead and drew her into an embrace, so warm and comforting. "Once, centuries ago, I used to be married to three women. You know the deities, Ọba, Ọṣun, and Ọya."

His voice had a solemn edge to it. She froze in his embrace. She wasn't sure why, but somehow, she was afraid of the story he was about to tell, and she didn't even know what it said. Maybe it was the mention of the deities, and the reminder of her own glaring mortality.

Ṣango lightly stroked her back, probably sensing the fear running through her, each stroke of his fingers sending warmth and light into her body.

"My marriage to Ọba was arranged. The details will bore you, but it was one of those necessary things done to save the world when it was still new and quite fragile," he continued when she had calmed down.

"The world is still fragile. It's always going to be fragile," she said against his skin.

"True. But back then, the spiritual bonds were still weak, and realms still leaked into one another. We gods were still new and young and arrogant, and we made a lot mistakes."

"You are still arrogant," she said, and he chuckled.

"Well, we still are." He had to agree. "Ọṣun was a relationship we did not expect to go any farther, and when it did, we both did not know what to do with it. But Ọya was my first love, and for centuries, my only love."

He paused as Toyin untangled herself from him and watched him carefully.

"What happened between you two?"

"Betrayal. One would think that as gods, we would be immune or even above feelings like jealousy, except we are not. We are worse than humans when it comes to such feelings. Timi Ọlọ́fà-iná and Gbonka were my best friends and generals, the ones I trusted completely. But they were polar opposites when it came to their characteristics. Timi was the master of the arrow of fire. He was hot-headed, he killed first and asked questions later. Gbonka was the voice of reasoning, the strategist. Now, maybe because we both had similar traits, Timi wanted my throne, the Kingdom of Oyo. He wanted my ability to command thunder, to breathe fire. In one of his plots, he set me up with Ọya, not knowing she was his lover, to learn my secrets and how to destroy me. The Baba Mogba learned of their plot and told me about it.

"I am giving you the short version of it. I was mad, so mad that I burned down my house. Thankfully, I did not hurt anyone. Well, Orí had the time of his life playing both Ọya and me because Ọya found out that Timi never truly loved her and had only been using her, so she cursed him to know nothing but hate. Which is how Timi and I found ourselves in this endless cycle."

He waited for Toyin to catch up. One look at her face told him she was riveted.

"After the fire I caused on my palace, Ọba and Ọṣun could not take it anymore. They ended our marriage contract and took their own path. I was so heartbroken that I might have faded into nothing, if not for Gbonka and the Baba Mogba who were with me all through. I do not think I would have survived. It was the first time my fire died, and I lay unconscious. Back then, it was shorter, but it could have been worse. Through the Baba Mogba's endless worship, I woke up again. Timi, now completely consumed by hate, tried to kill me the very first moment I stepped out into the open after I woke up. However, Gbonka saw him first and took an arrow of fire in his heart for me. Enraged, I killed Timi, but that was when Olódùmarè decided They had had enough of our nonsense and deemed the world of deities and humans to be separated. But not before Timi and Gbonka both got their demi-god and immortality status. Both of them are tethered to me, one fuelled by his hate for me and the other by his love."

She was still following his tale when he checked.

"After the separation, the Baba Mogba were distraught to be separated from me, and somehow, they withered away."

***

"My mum is a descendant of the Baba Mogba," Toyin said when Ṣango paused, and to her surprise, she felt a strange sense of pride that she belonged to a people who had been with Ṣango at the time.

"Is she?" Ṣango replied, the surprise in his tone unmistakeable. "It makes sense now."

"What does?"

"If your mother is from the lineage of Baba Mogba cult, then you are, too. Strong and ancient power runs through your veins, although mightily diluted due to generations of intermarriage with the ordinary humans. It explains why your mind is still intact after your encounter with Timi. It explains so much more than that. You are from the clan of the people who saved my life." His amber eyes flashed, as if he had a newfound respect for her.

"Oh," she said.

"You keep giving me new reasons to love you every day."

Toyin started. She hadn't been expecting him to say that. It clarified what she thought she'd heard him say when they had sex the first time.

"Love... You love me?"

"Hmm," Ṣango confirmed. "That is what complicated this whole thing. My fire went out the minute I confirmed how I feel about you. It reminded me of the pain I had felt once before and what I could feel again, if something happened to you."

"Ṣango... I..."

"Relax." He smiled. "I am not going to burden you with this."

His tone sounded kind of sad, and Toyin felt a lump rising in her throat.

Ṣango stroked her forehead. "I know loving you and wanting to keep you by my side is selfish and unfair to you. I am a deity, and you are human even if you have the blood of a powerful people running through your veins. So, I am going to bear the burden of loving you alone. I shall fix this mess and stop the world from ending, and you will get to live your life to the fullest and achieve the things you want to achieve."

"Wait… what are you saying?" The lump in her throat thickened. "You are coming back, aren't you?"

"Once everything gets sorted out, there will not be a need for me to come back. The world will be fixed, and everything will be returned to normal, and you can have a normal life here."

"A normal life." She repeated the words, three completely mundane words that somehow felt burdensome and heavy.

"It is all you have ever wanted, and I shall do everything I can to make that possible for you. It is the only way I can love you without getting either of us hurt."

"Yes, it's all I have ever wanted," she concurred.

Ṣango was right. What they had, what they shared, was not something that could take them anywhere without unnecessary detrimental sacrifices, and that was exactly what she didn't want. But why did she feel so sad? Why were tears threatening to spill out? Why did her throat hurt so much from the effort it was taking to fight back her tears?

"So, this is goodbye?"

"I have thought about a million ways to do this, but I did not think it would hurt like this. I do not think I—"

Toyin couldn't listen anymore. "Sometimes, words aren't enough to explain how we feel, and sometimes, the words are just too hurtful to speak or listen to. So, let's just not talk." She then kissed him.

In place of words, they made love slowly, taking their time to taste, to feel, and to memorise every inch of each other's bodies. When they climaxed, it was powerful and as sad as goodbyes were between lovers.

Toyin woke the next morning to an empty bed. She ran her fingers over the sheets and it was still warm. He'd only just left. She flew out of bed and ran out of the bedroom. Maybe she could catch up to him. There were things she had to say, things she should have said to him to him the previous night. Yet, even as she did so, she knew it was a futile effort. Ṣango didn't travel like humans did. He was probably already back in Ìlú Òrìṣà.

I love you were the words he had whispered into her ear when he climaxed, words she'd pretended not to hear because she had been too afraid of what it would mean for her and the choice she would have to make if she had declared that she loved him, too.

But now, stepping back into the apartment, even with furniture and fixtures still in place, it felt empty. She sat on the floor, the coolness of the tiles biting into her bare skin, and began to cry. She opened the floodgates of tears she should have shed while he was with her, and now, she was never going to see him again. Not even when she died. She wouldn't see him because their paths had now been separated forever.

CHAPTER TWENTY-THREE

It had been almost two weeks since Ṣango had left. The thirty days deadline given to him had passed, and seeing as the world was still standing, she guessed he had been able to fix the problem. The days had gone by slowly and painfully. Toyin realised she would give anything to feel his presence in her mind again.

She had spent the time they were together telling him no. Still, she wasn't going to regret anything. It was the one promise she had made to herself that she intended to keep, and he wouldn't want her to either. Not like he no longer existed — the world was still beating, which meant he had found his Oṣé, he had defeated Timi, and everything was in back in place as it should be.

Their paths should never have crossed, but they had, and it had been the happiest moments of her life. Even now, she was still happy, knowing he was out there somewhere. She had even seen Ṣeye. He'd come to the hospital where she worked with his mother for her monthly check up. The weird thing was that neither of them knew who she was. It was as if she had been wiped completely out of their memories.

Toyin wasn't upset about it, not in the very least, because of all the bad things that could have happened to him, losing his memory of her was the least. Good thing his mother didn't remember her, too. It made things a lot easier.

After Ṣango had left, she had moved into his apartment because it made her feel less lonely, and she had finally gathered the courage to apply to study neurosurgery. Ṣango had left so she could live the life she wanted, and she wouldn't disappoint him. She went back to work a week before her leave ended.

She was happier, she laughed a lot more, and even for the first time accepted to go on a girls' night out with her colleagues, Lola and Nkem. They were the closest she had to friends in the hospital, but she had always drawn a line with them. Still, she was living a wholesome life now, so it wouldn't hurt to actually have girlfriends.

So when Nkem had asked earlier that day, during their morning rounds, "It's the first time we are all free together, there are no surgeries fixed for this evening, and since it's Friday, Lola and I are having a girls' night out. Would you like to come with us?" she had said yes. Nkem, who really hadn't been expecting her to agree, didn't even try to hide her surprise. As soon as they got back to their station, she announced to Lola and everybody within the vicinity that Toyin was going out with them that evening.

"What happened? I am going to kill a cow today and offer it to the gods. This one said you are going out with us today." Lola laughed and clapped her hands.

Her comment about killing a cow to offer the gods reminded her of Ṣango's aversion to human sacrifice, and she laughed.

"There's something different about you. I noticed it when you came back. Like when you were applying for your leave, you looked like you were carrying the burden of the whole world on your shoulders. Even a widow would have looked happier than you did, and then you came back with this glow up, and you are always laughing, and now you want to go out with us. To be honest, I thought you didn't like us o. There was always—"

"Ah ah, Lola! It's enough enh, she finally agreed to go out with us today, and you want to scare her away with too much talk."

"What? Leave me, you know I like to talk, abeg," she said to Nkem and turned back to face Toyin.

Nkem sighed and mouthed the word 'sorry' to her, then went to sort out some files on the desk—their hospital, like many others in the country, still preferred the old school filing system as opposed to being computerised.

"Me, I know where the glow is coming from. You broke up with your stiff-necked boyfriend that usually comes here to pick you up. I saw how you two were ignoring each other the other day when he came to the hospital."

"Lola!" Nkem and one other nurse, an older woman, called at the same time.

"What is it nau?"

"It's not everything you notice that you must say." The older nurse kissed her teeth and grabbed a file from the counter and handed it to her. "Go and give this to Dr Ifediora. He asked for it a couple of minutes ago."

"Yes, ma," Lola said as she begrudgingly collected the file and went on the errand.

Toyin had only laughed as Lola left. It was true she had considered Lola a bit too loud and Nkem a bit too complacent in tolerating her friend's behaviour, though deep down, the truth was she wished they had included her in their gossip. But it wasn't their fault—she was the one had been distant. And now, all of that was changing. She was living not just for herself but for Ṣango, as well, who she suspected was watching her from where he was.

That night for their date night, which began at an exotic restaurant, she had chosen a turquoise mini flare dress, completely open at the back and showing a little cleavage. She had imagined Ṣango's amber eyes watching her as she dressed, imagined his hands peeling the dress off her before laying her flat on her back and then doing crazy things to her with his mouth.

She realised only seconds later she had slid out of her dress. Knowing there was no hope for it, she sat down at the edge of the bed and spread her legs and lightly began to stroke herself. Imagining Ṣango watching her, she stroked faster and faster until she came. The release was a much needed one yet nothing compared to what he would have given her.

She smiled to herself when she finally stepped out of the house for her date with the girls. She looked skywards just before getting into her Uber and said, "You have completely ruined me for other men." She could have sworn she saw a faint flash of lightning across the sky.

After dinner with the girls, Lola had the insane idea to go clubbing.

"I can't remember the last time I went to a club. What are we supposed to do there?" Nkem protested, and Toyin nodded in agreement as they stepped out of the restaurant.

"You will scream when the DJ plays a song you like, jump up and down, drink, dance, what else do they do at a nightclub enh, Nkem?" Lola replied.

"But we can do all that your house nau, like the last time," Nkem countered. Again, Toyin agreed although she didn't know about the last time since she hadn't been there.

"I don't think I'm in the mood to bump into strangers with sweaty bodies and excessive loud music," she said.

"Thank you!" Nkem said.

"Fine, na wa for the two of sha let's take the party home instead," Lola conceded. "But it's your house we are going, you know my landlady hates me, small thing now, she will give me quit notice. You know how hard it is to find correct house in this Lagos."

This gave Toyin an insane idea. "Let's go to my house instead. I have an insane sound system, and someone I know left behind a massive collection of wine and liquor. We don't have to spend any extra money, and we can have all the fun we want."

"Osheyyyy, I tell you say lowkey this geh na street she just dey form for that hospital," Lola screamed.

"You are so silly. Sha let's go." Toyin was standing in the middle of the girls and linked arms with them and walked to car park where their Uber was waiting for them.

Half an hour later, they were in the apartment, and the girls couldn't hide their surprise and excitement.

"Welcome to my humble abode," Toyin said and gave a cliché bow and then spotted Mr Panda. "Meet Mr Panda, my housemate." She swung the giant panda off the couch and hung it on her waist. "Mr Panda, my friends, Lola and Nkem."

Nkem laughed, and Lola held the panda's paws and shook it. "Hello, Mr Panda," she said, and they all burst out laughing.

"But wait o, did you do… wetin that girl call am for inside that Sugar Rush feem…?

"Ritualism" Nkem answered as she took a seat on the luxurious couch.

"Ehen! Did you do ritualism when you went on leave? Look at this place nauu. And it doesn't look like it from outside."

Toyin laughed. "If I did money rituals, I won't be here with you people abeg."

"Abi you have sugar daddy ni?" Nkem chipped in.

"Hmmm." She shrugged, leaving the answer to Nkem's question open. The girls stared at her open-mouthed. "Close your mouths jor. How I got this place is a long story that I don't want to get into today."

"Okay o, me I kuku like enjoyment. I'm all for the soft life." Lola plopped on a couch and leaned to pick up the TV remote.

"Abeg bring the drinks let us—"

Whatever Nkem was about to say was interrupted by the sound of the doorbell. Toyin stared at the door, puzzled. She wasn't expecting anybody. The caretaker wouldn't even talk to her ever since she'd moved into Ṣango's apartment— he avoided her as if she had two heads.

"That's odd," she said, a sense of foreboding hitting her as she walked to the door. The atmosphere suddenly didn't feel right.

Taking in a deep breath, she opened the door to find Gbonka standing outside.

She heaved a sigh of relief upon finding it was just him, and then she panicked. If he was here, then Ṣango wasn't far away, and the melancholia on Gbonka's face scared her. He hadn't said a word yet, but she knew something was terribly, terribly wrong.

"Girls," she called without taking her eyes off Gbonka, who looked every bit human in a T-shirt and jeans. "I'm sorry, but you have to—"

She didn't even need to complete her sentence as both Nkem and Lola were by her side with their purses and shoes in their hands.

"We'll call you when we get home," Nkem said, and Lola nodded. They both had an apologetic look in their eyes.

At first, she didn't understand. She was the one who should be apologising, then she remembered their earlier sugar daddy conversation. She wondered, as Gbonka stepped aside for them to pass, what it was about him that made them think he could be her sponsor. Then it clicked.

Gbonka might pale when compared to Ṣango, but he was still an outwardly handsome being, and he had that same authoritative arrogance

Ṣango had, although Ṣango's could be multiplied by a million and it still wouldn't measure up.

When the girls had left, Gbonka stepped into the apartment and shut the door behind him. "I used the doorbell because I sensed their presence, and I did not want to alarm them."

"I know, I understand. Ṣango can come in now, they are gone," she said, looking around expectantly for Ṣango to appear. Even though she knew his appearance meant something had gone wrong with whatever plan he'd had, she was still excited and, truthfully, happy that he was back.

"He is not here."

"What do you mean, he isn't here?" she asked, and even before Gbonka spoke, she dreaded what he would say next.

"Ṣango has done something really, really foolish," Gbonka said.

Toyin's heart plummeted to the pit of her stomach.

CHAPTER TWENTY-FOUR

"What do you mean? How… I thought…"

"We do not have much time, so here is the short version of what happened. Ṣango sought an audience with Olódùmarè himself and made a bargain. To skip the whole process and for the return of his Oṣé, he asked for one final battle with Timi. If he wins, the Oṣé will be returned to him, the world would be safe, and most importantly, you will be safe."

"I knew he had a plan, but this is nothing out of the ordinary —"

"Of course, he knew Olódùmarè would say the same thing, and that is when he made the stupid bargain."

"What did he do?" Toyin said the words one after the other slowly.

"He is going to fight Timi as a human."

"What?" Her eyes widened in horror.

"He asked that Olódùmarè strip him of his powers so that he fights as a human."

"Timi's powers will be taken away, too?"

Gbonka shook his head. "His powers remain, being an advantage over Ṣango, the advantage he has always wanted. If Timi wins, all Ṣango's authority and power goes to him, and he gets what he has been coveting. He becomes a god. Trust me, nobody wants that to happen, not the deities, not humans, and not even Olódùmarè."

"Then why would They allow that to happen? Olódùmarè, They are the Supreme, They have control over everything. Why did They agree to something like this?"

"Because balance is needed for the preservation of the world. Why did you think Timi had to die? It is because Gbonka died. He died because of his intense love for Ṣango, and to create balance, Timi had to die, too, because he hates Ṣango. Hate took away his Oṣé, love has to bring it back. But since love failed to do that, he has to fight for what is truly his. He must prove his worthiness by fighting Timi as a human, then he gets his Oṣé back, he gets to protect the woman he loves and keep his throne. But it is at the great risk of losing everything. The risk is what keeps the balance."

Toyin touched her pulsing temples at the onslaught of a headache. She rubbed them to ease the pain. "This is all so... why would he do something like this?"

"For you, Toyin. For you. When a deity loves, they love hard and deep."

The words hit her deep into her soul. He was doing this for her, and she was here living her life, enjoying it even without thinking of —

"Only you can help him," Gbonka said, disrupting her thoughts.

Toyin's legs were weak. She leaned against the wall for support. She had to stop Ṣango from making such a stupid mistake. It was all her fault in the first place, that she couldn't admit her love for him, that she couldn't die for him.

But the truth was she was only happy living because she knew Ṣango was alive, that he was watching over her somewhere and somehow. If he no longer existed, then her life would be meaningless, too. It would be worse than when her father had died. Back then, she hadn't had any control over her father's life. Things were different now. She was no ordinary woman — she was a descendant of power, she was a woman in love, and she would do anything to save the man she loved.

"What do I have to do?" she asked, determination fuelling her reasoning.

"He is currently locked in Àjalẹ̀ ẹsín, the only place powerful enough to contain a deity. It is a place bound by powerful magic that strips a deity of their power. He has to stay there for two weeks. In those two weeks, the world will be kept as it is, but everything will change depending on who wins the final match."

This all sounded so dire.

Gbonka continued. "Like I said, nobody wants this, especially the deities. They feel it is a slight, a disrespect to them for a demi-god to become a god. He could be used as entertainment, for their amusement, but they do not want him as one of them. Ṣango has less than twenty-four hours before all his powers are gone and he is no better than a human. We need to get him out of there, but none of the ethereal beings can do it. They cannot risk going into Àjalẹ̀ ẹ̀sín and getting trapped in there. But you are human. You can get him out of there. You are warded against the evils of that place."

"And what's in it for you?" Toyin asked.

His eyes widened first in confusion and then in surprise and finally in concession. "I keep forgetting how strong-willed you are. How did you figure it out?"

"In your carefully planned ruse, you slipped up and referred to Gbonka in the third person. So, answer the question. Why do you want to get Ṣango out? It is all to your advantage if he fights as a human, Timi."

"Oh, dear, Toyin. Ṣango has never, ever been an ordinary human. Stripping him of his powers does not make him a less formidable enemy, but that is beside the point. What I cannot stand is the insult. Ìlú Òrìṣà thinks I cannot defeat Ṣango in his full element, and I want to prove them wrong. I will destroy him and take everything he has ever had and owned and then I can finally be happy and find peace."

Toyin snickered. "That will never happen. And I'm sure deep down you know it. Even if you defeat Ṣango, you are cursed to only know hate. When there is no one left to hate, you will begin to hate yourself. You will be so consumed by it that it will overcome you and destroy you."

"You have no idea what you are talking about. Ṣango's woman or not, you are nothing but an ordinary human."

She sighed. "I want to feel bad for you, but I can't. You brought the curse on yourself, played with a woman's heart, and got yourself into this mess." And with a wave of her hand as if dismissing him, she added, "What did you do to dear Gbonka?"

"Nothing. I only borrowed his likeness. He is probably off somewhere sulking and fuming about his lord's situation."

"Hmm." She nodded. "I guess he's too powerful for you to take over his body. I'm curious to know what you actually look like."

"I see. He has made you his woman, and now, you no longer fear. You are coming with me, whether you like it or not."

"Stop insulting me. Yes, I am Ṣango's woman, but you can say it without sounding so condescending. I am in a position only goddesses have ever been. So, you will speak to me with respect, and I never said I wasn't going with you. I'd like to see you destroyed with my own eyes."

Timi was taken aback by the intensity in her gaze, but he recovered quickly and then grabbed her hand, causing them to dissolve into a fog of dark mist.

Toyin felt herself floating through a cloud of darkness for about ten seconds before she felt her feet touch the ground. The fog cleared just as slowly as she released her breath. Timi let go of her hand, and she looked around her. They stood at the entrance of a cave, the darkness and hollowness of it making her swallow nervously. So in contrast to the beauty of the pale pink evening sky over them. Time must be slower here because it was almost midnight when they had left her apartment in the human world.

Everything felt different—the air, the dark sand on the ground, with bits of rock spread about on what looked like a deserted land. She felt so out of place in her gown she hadn't even thought of changing.

"This is the entrance to Àjalè èsín, the dungeon of shame," Timi said.

The deep, gruff voice, so much different from Gbonka's smooth baritone, brought her attention the bald-headed man with the heavily bearded face. He had a tattoo of seven tiny flames under his eyes, four on his left and three on his right, caramel-skinned and in a black sleeveless kaftan and gypsy pants. A bow was slung across his chest, and Toyin assumed the quiver contained the infamous arrows of fire. She had to admit he was way more handsome than she had expected him to be. He looked every bit as dangerously handsome as a Viking.

"Like what you see?" he said cockily as he noticed her appraisal of him.

Toyin only bared her teeth in a mock smile. She was in his territory now; she had to choose her words carefully before one of those arrows of fire found its way into her heart. She cut her eyes back to the entrance of the cave and looked back at the darkness that seemed ready to draw her in and consume her.

"Ṣango is in there?" she asked, seeking confirmation.

Timi nodded slowly, but underneath the cool demeanour he was trying to show her lay some sort of eagerness. She detected it in the way he avoided looking directly at the cave, as if he were trying to show her the cave didn't unnerve him.

The more she moved towards the entrance, the more focused on her he seemed. Yet, the closer she was to the cave, the more she felt her soul being drawn from her. He'd said humans were warded against the cave's power, but if the cave had this effect on her and she wasn't yet inside it, how much torture was Ṣango going through inside?

She took in a deep breath. For him, for the man she loved, she would go in there. Just one more step, and she would be completely engulfed in the darkness of the cave.

"Toyin!"

She whipped her head about at the sound of her name and saw Ṣango emerging out of a circle of red cloud, followed closely by Gbonka. Another circle of dark cloud opened and a woman — no, a goddess — stepped out, dressed in dark green tunic, her hair darker than the night and flowing all the way to her ankles. In her hand, she held a staff as dark as her hair. Upon a closer look, Toyin realised her hair *was* her staff. And she found she couldn't keep looking at her — it was more draining than peering at the dark cave.

"Ọya!" Timi called in surprise as the woman sauntered towards him.

Ọya. This was the goddess who had betrayed Ṣango and who had in turn been betrayed by Timi. Goosebumps travelled up her skin.

"What is going on here?" Toyin asked, looking from Ṣango to Timi.

"Ah, this bastard." Timi strung his bow, and immediately, the arrow he nocked blazed up. He pointed it at Toyin. "Keep walking. Do not stop until you get into that cave."

"Toyin, do not dare take another step," Ṣango thundered. The sky and the earth shook as his eyes blazed.

The fear Toyin had been trying to resist rushed to the surface as the understanding of what was happening came to her. Ṣango was obviously not in Àjalẹ̀ ẹ̀sín. She had been bait to draw him out and get him trapped inside the cave.

Her eyes caught a glimpse of Ọya, who stood to the side expressionless, waiting. Despite herself, she couldn't help but think of how beautiful she was. Damn, were there no ugly deities?

"This is between us. I warned you not to touch her," Ṣango bellowed.

She could have sworn she saw sparks fly out his mouth. Timi must have seen it, too, because he dropped his weapon and immediately pulled Toyin to him, positioning her in front of him, although they were now several steps away from the entrance of the cave. She could still feel the darkness trying to suck her in. As Timi tightened his arm around her neck, she struggled against his grip but had to be mindful to not topple them both into the entrance of the cave.

"Go ahead, you fire-breathing monster. Go ahead, burn me, I dare you." Ṣango stilled and put out a hand, ordering Gbonka not to move.

"You brought her here? Knowing what it means for Ọya and I to meet again?" Timi spat, the strain and fear in his voice not to be mistaken.

"You brought this on yourself, Timi. You chose not to play fair. This is costing me a lot, but you are going with Ọya," Ṣango said, his eyes not leaving Toyin's.

"You are coming with me. You do not have a choice," Ọya said, speaking for the first time. Her voice was surprisingly soft for the goddess of death and the guardian of the underworld.

"What did he offer you to make you do this?"

"He called in a favour, a very dangerous favour," Ọya answered and nonchalantly blew out dirt from her fingernails. "I do not like either of you, but I hate you more than I hate him. So, it gives me great pleasure to do this."

Toyin's fear tripled. What kind of deal had Ṣango gotten himself in? She however didn't have time to process her questions when Timi's next words shocked her.

"I will not go down alone. If I am going with you, then she is coming with me," he said and pulled them both into the dark hollowness of the cave.

The last thing Toyin saw as her screams were swallowed up by the darkness wasn't Ọya's insidious smile but Ṣango jumping into the cave after them—after her, engulfed in mad fury as flames took over his body.

CHAPTER TWENTY-FIVE

Toyin knew she was dead when she saw her father smiling at her and waving her to him. He was sitting on a bench in a garden of light, a newspaper open in his hand. The woods around them provided them with warmth. He was just as she remembered him when she was a child. His moustache twitched as he smiled at her.

But just as she started to walk towards him, he dissolved into nothingness, and in his place was her grandmother as she had been when she was young.

She knew it was her grandmother even though she had never met her when she was alive because the woman was the exact replica of her in the white silk dress she was wearing. She exuded so much warmth, even more than the trees, and her gap-toothed smiled made Toyin feel at home. Again, as she started to walk towards her, the woman shook her head, still smiling.

"This is not your place. Go back, he is waiting for you," she said, pointing at something behind Toyin.

Toyin looked back in the direction her grandmother was pointing, and that's when she heard him call her name. His voice was desperate, pleading, yet what made the call irresistible was the love—heavy, whole, and true.

She turned away from her grandmother, and at first, she started walking, then she was jogging, and then she was running towards him, towards her love, her man, her life.

***

She opened her eyes, and the first person she saw was Ṣango who heaved a sigh of relief and pulled her into hug. She smiled and hugged him back, pulling him tighter, and she began to cry.

"I love you so much… I'm so sorry. It's all my fault. I love you, I love you." She sobbed against his shoulders.

"I know, I know, and I love you, too, so much more than I can explain."

"Oh, please, do we also have to stay to watch this?" Ọya's deceptively soft voice broke them apart.

Ṣango stood up slowly and turned to face Ọya, but not before he lovingly stroked her face. That's when Toyin took notice of where she was. To describe the bedroom as grand would be an understatement—the entire apartment building where she lived looked like a hut compared to this. The luxurious bedroom resembled something out of the Roman Empire. The bed was so soft, she wanted to sink further into it and bury herself in the silk sheets that awed her. But the two beyond beautiful women who stood side by side in the centre of the room prevented her from doing just that.

One she recognised as Ọya. The other, she assumed was another goddess she didn't know. She also didn't fail to notice that Gbonka was standing as far away from the goddesses as he could, and he looked like he wanted to be anywhere but in that room.

"So, this is the woman who caused all the fuss," the other goddess said, eyeing Toyin.

"Ọṣun, please be respectful!" Ṣango groaned his warning.

"Oh, if she can risk going into Àjalẹ̀ ẹ̀sín, though a foolish thing, it takes only the strongest willed to do that, and for it, she has all my respect," Ọṣun said.

"Plus, she puts up with your insufferable ass, and I owe her ancestors an apology for separating them and their lord," Ọya added.

Toyin sat up straighter. She was in the company of two of the greatest deities ever, and she had nothing to say.

"Shut it, the both of you."

"We had a deal," Ọya said, the bored expression returning to her tone.

Ṣango put his hand in his pocket, brought out an oval-shaped stone, and tossed it to her. She caught it in one swift motion and smiled.

"That is a very precious thing I am giving you. Make sure you return it to me in one piece," Ṣango warned.

"Hmm," was the only response he got from Ọya as she twirled the stone in her hand and it slowly disappeared.

"And I have seen that the human is alive and well, and by permission of Olódùmarè, your Oṣé will be returned to you," Ọya said.

As she spoke the word, a silver-bladed double axe, the size and length of a sword, materialised in Ṣango's hand, the wooden handle thickly crooked, with ancient markings she couldn't read carved into it. He closed his eyes, and Toyin could almost feel the pleasure that ran through him as his hands closed around the weapon.

"Finally," he said.

"Now that our business here is done, shall we?" Ọṣun said as she and Ọya turned to leave. Ọṣun paused and said to Toyin, "If you ever get tired of him, or he messes with you, there is room for three in our company," she said and winked at her.

"That is never going to happen. How did you two become friends, anyway?" Ṣango said, putting a protective arm on Toyin.

"What, you think we would spend the rest of eternity fighting over a man we both are not married to anymore? What a waste of a life," Ọya answered him, still with the bored tone.

"Besides, we found we have a likening for human parties and similar taste in human men," Ọṣun added, and Ṣango rolled his eyes as they both left the room.

Toyin, who had been watching the whole exchange, laughed as Gbonka released a breath of relief.

"I am glad to see you alive and well, Toyin," he said with a genuine smile at her. "But I shall leave you to do whatever it is you want to do to each other now," he said, bowed to Ṣango, and left.

Ṣango sat down beside her. His weapon had now reduced drastically in size, as small as the stone he had given Ọya. He slipped it easily into his pocket. Then, he pulled Toyin in for another hug. She noticed for the first time that she was wearing a night dress that left nothing to be imagined.

He chuckled. "That is a gift from Ọṣun."

Toyin laughed.

Ṣango filled her in on what had happened. He had indeed made a bargain to have his powers stripped in a battle with Timi, where Timi would still have his powers. But it didn't involve him being locked up in Àjalẹ̀ ẹsín, a dreadful place even the most powerful deities dread. All Olódùmarè had to do was speak away his powers.

"So, why did Timi..." Toyin asked.

"Timi has always been insecure. That insecurity was what ignited his hatred for me.

Even with my powers gone, he still did not feel confident enough to defeat me, and so he tried to use you as a bait to get me trapped in Àjalè èsín because he knew I would come after you know matter what. And that sacrifice we made was what saved us."

"I don't understand." Toyin shook her head slightly.

"Hate started the whole mess, so love had to clean it up," Ṣango said with a smile. "You love me enough to want to die for me, and I loved you enough to risk eternal torment by jumping into Àjalè èsín, a place of eternal torment and pain. The power of the love we both share pushed us out of the cave. Ọya collected Timi's soul and took it to the underworld, I got my Oṣé back, and we get to live."

"I didn't know I was going to die if I entered that cave. Timi told me humans were warded against the powers of the cave and —"

"Tell me, did you honestly believe as you stood at the entrance that you would come out of there alive?" Ṣango asked in all seriousness.

Toyin shook her head slowly in response because she could not trust herself to speak. The truth was, she knew, she'd felt it in her spirits as she stood at the entrance, that she would not make it out alive.

"So what happens now? Everything's sorted, and we have to be separated again? This is why I couldn't bring myself to say the word. Even though I love you so much, it sometimes hurts. The fact that we have to go our separate ways scares me. The past few weeks were tough on me. I had to make myself happy because it is what you would have wanted, but truthfully, that happiness didn't feel complete. There was a longing, a waiting… I know, I know, I am such a selfish person, but if I had admitted to you how much I truly loved you, then I would not have survived our separation, and I know now that I have admitted it, I'll go back and try to live my best life yet it will never ever feel complete, not without you by my side."

Toyin left the tears flow down her cheeks, and when Ṣango tried to cup her face, she brushed him away, unable to bring herself to look at him.

"Look at me, Órèkelèwá. Please," he begged. "Wanting to be loved the way you want is not selfish. I understand how important your life as a human is to you, how important your dreams are to you, which is why I made another bargain with Olódùmarè."

Toyin slowly lifted her eyes to him.

"What did you do again?" Her voice was laced with fear that he must have taken a stupid risk once more.

"Deities are not allowed to live in the human realm, which is also my fault. But we can visit from time to time. So I asked that I be allowed to spend the rest of your life with you in the human realm, but I shall live with you as a human. My powers will not be taken but will lay dormant inside me, and my duties will be temporarily transferred to Gbonka. This can only be broken the day you die."

"What?" She couldn't believe what she was hearing. This was such a huge sacrifice Ṣango was making for her.

"Yes, Toyin." He wiped her tears and lifted her head. "Until the day you die, I will be by your side, loving you, cheering you on, and making you happy. Do not get this wrong, this is not a sacrifice. I am doing this because I want to, and I will do this every time you are reborn into the world."

"I'll find you every time I come back, and I'll love you even more each time. That's a promise I intend to keep for all my lives. I love you so much, Ṣango Olúkòsó akata yẹri yẹri Àrábámbí Ọkọ mi."

"What are you…" Ṣango's eyes flashed—he couldn't resist the head-swelling effect hearing his Oríkì from the mouth of the woman he loved had on him.

Toyin smiled as she realised what was happening. Learning his Oríkì that night had definitely been a good idea. She got to her knees without ceasing her chant, her see-through nightdress riding to her thighs.

She pushed Ṣango down on his back and strode him.

"Iná l'ójú, iná l'ẹnu Eègún tin'yọná lẹnu. Òrìṣà ti nbologbó lẹrù …"

Ṣango could not hold back anymore. He pulled her to him and crushed his lips against hers. She kissed him back for a while and then pulled away from him, laughing.

"That's not how this is going to work, my love," she said, grinding her groin against him. And even through the layers of his robe, she felt his cock jolt against her inner thighs. "I told you that next time, I'll explore every inch and corner of your body."

"Ah, this woman," was all Ṣango could manage as she began to rid him little by little of his clothes, planting kisses here and there.

Only when he was completely naked did she rid herself of her flimsy nightdress. Then, she positioned herself on his cock, and as she sank down and began to ride him, she bent over to kiss him, taking his moans into her mouth. When she climaxed, he flipped her over so that she lay on her back. Without detaching himself from her, he pinched her clit as he continued to thrust into her, and when she climaxed again, this time, he climaxed with her.

She kissed him deeply. Her mother had been right—she was no ordinary woman. She was a woman who loved and was loved by a god in this life and in the next.

"I love you," Ṣango whispered into her ear, like he had done the first time they'd made love.

This time, she didn't pretend she hadn't heard it.

"I know, and I love you, too," she whispered back and snuggled into him.

He wrapped his arms around her, and she felt safe and happy as she knew she would feel for the rest of her life.

Thank you for reading Amber Fire by Aminat Sanni-Kamal. If you enjoyed this story, please leave a review on the site of purchase.

AUTHOR'S NOTE:

Dear Reader,

Thank you for purchasing and reading Amber Fire.

As an avid fan of Yoruba mythology, I had so much fun writing this story. Retelling Sango's folklore and the relationship between his wives and generals proved a little challenging because there are many stories about Sango ultimately saying the same thing. I wanted a clear distinction between the other stories and this one without straying too far away from the myths and lore about Sango.

Another challenge was writing Yoruba words with the appropriate tonal marks. As a teenager in secondary school, I was fluent in reading and writing Yoruba. But, at some point, I lost my touch. When I decided to write Amber Fire, I knew the story would feel incomplete if the words weren't written properly. I considered outsourcing it but decided against it and tried my rusty hands at it. It turned out to be fun writing Yoruba with accents and marks again.

I also slightly tweaked Sango's Oriki to suit Toyin's purpose in Amber Fire in the final chapter.

It is very important to mention that though this story is heavily based on Yoruba myths and lore, it is largely fiction — most places, names, and items are products of my imagination. This book is also a result of my love for Korean fantasy dramas and Yoruba mythology - like 10% Kfantasy and 90% Yoruba mythology.

In all, as much as it was fun writing it, a lot of research and self-doubt when into its production. But I am so in love with the end result, and I hope this book has, in one way or the other, brought a smile to your face and made you happy. I look forward to your reviews and thoughts.

Xoxo,
Aminat

AUTHOR BIO:

Aminat Sanni-Kamal is a passionate African romance and fantasy writer. Born and raised in Nigeria, her deep appreciation for the vibrant Yoruba culture and the rich folklore of her homeland is evident in every word she pens.

With a heart captivated by the intricacies of human connections, Aminat infuses her stories with soulful romance, vivid settings, and the timeless allure of African traditions. Drawing inspiration from the magic of Yoruba mythology, she transports readers into a world where love transcends time and space.

When she's not crafting stories that make hearts flutter, Aminat can be found immersed in the pages of books from various genres, constantly seeking new avenues of inspiration or simply enjoying a good book. She's also an avid fan of Korean dramas, indulging in tales of romance and drama from distant lands.

Through her writing, Aminat aspires to share the beauty of African culture, and the power of love, with readers around the world. Her unique blend of passion, culture, and imagination promises to leave an indelible mark in the hearts of those who embark on the journeys she creates.

Social Media Links:

Instagram: https://www.instagram.com/aminatsannik/
Twitter: https://twitter.com/aminatsannik
Youtube: https://www.youtube.com/channel/UCv_LyH L73F6bQRk_UoyTn1A
Newsletter: https://aminatsannikamal.substack.com/

OTHER BOOKS BY LOVE AFRICA PRESS

Dating Mr Famous by Glory Abah
Rough Diamond by Kiru Taye
Falling for Her Bad Boy Boss by Zee Monodee
Love and Handicrafts by Nana Prah

CONNECT WITH US

Facebook.com/LoveAfricaPress
Twitter.com/LoveAfricaPress
Instagram.com/LoveAfricaPress

SIGN UP TO OUR NEWSLETTER

https://www.loveafricapress.com/newsletter

www.ingramcontent.com/pod-product-compliance
Lightning Source LLC
Chambersburg PA
CBHW071149180726
48291CB00007B/2392